THE OFFICE GRAPEVINE

Barrington Corporation News Bulletin
Vol.1 No. 2
February 1999

• The rumors are true! Olivia McGovern is pregnant and sources say that dashing lawyer Lucas Hunter was seen kissing the pretty paralegal under the mistletoe at the company Christmas party a few months ago. Could *he* be the baby's father?

• And, is anyone else wondering who the mysterious Rex Barrington III is? After all, no one has laid eyes on him, and he fired his assistant over the phone. All we know for sure is that those who have spoken to him say he has the sexiest voice.

• Finally, there's no gossip juicier than this statement overheard from Molly Doyle about her boss—"Sometimes, when he speaks at a departmental meeting, I think he's asking me to marry him." Does sweet Molly have a chance at hooking Jack Cavanaugh, one of Barrington's most eligible bachelors?

Dear Reader,

Happy Valentine's Day! What better way to celebrate than with a Silhouette Romance novel? We're sweeter than chocolate—and less damaging to the hips! This month is filled with special treats just for you. LOVING THE BOSS, our six-book series about office romances that lead to happily ever after, continues with *The Night Before Baby* by Karen Rose Smith. In this sparkling story, an unforgettable one-night stand—during the company Christmas party!—leads to an unexpected pregnancy and a must-read marriage of convenience.

Teresa Southwick crafts an emotional BUNDLES OF JOY title, in which the forbidden man of her dreams becomes a pregnant woman's stand-in groom. Don't miss *A Vow, a Ring, a Baby Swing.* When a devil-may-care bachelor discovers he's a daddy, he offers the prim heroine a chance to hold a *Baby in Her Arms,* as Judy Christenberry's LUCKY CHARM SISTERS trilogy resumes.

Award-winning author Marie Ferrarella proves it's *Never Too Late for Love* as the bride's mother and the groom's widower father discover their children's wedding was just the beginning in this charming continuation of LIKE MOTHER, LIKE DAUGHTER. Beloved author Arlene James lends a traditional touch to Silhouette Romance's ongoing HE'S MY HERO promotion with *Mr. Right Next Door.* And FAMILY MATTERS spotlights new talent Elyssa Henry with her heartwarming debut, *A Family for the Sheriff.*

Treat yourself to each and every offering this month. And in future months, look for more of the stories you love…and the authors you cherish.

Enjoy!

Mary-Theresa Hussey

Mary-Theresa Hussey
Senior Editor, Silhouette Romance

Please address questions and book requests to:
Silhouette Reader Service
U.S.: 3010 Walden Ave., P.O. Box 1325, Buffalo, NY 14269
Canadian: P.O. Box 609, Fort Erie, Ont. L2A 5X3

THE NIGHT BEFORE BABY

Karen Rose Smith

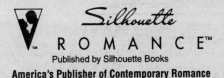
Silhouette
ROMANCE™
Published by Silhouette Books
America's Publisher of Contemporary Romance

To my cousin, Paul Arcuri,
my "expert" on small planes.

Special thanks and acknowledgment to Karen Rose Smith
for her contribution to the Loving the Boss series.

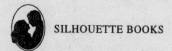 SILHOUETTE BOOKS

ISBN 0-373-19348-3

THE NIGHT BEFORE BABY

Copyright © 1999 by Harlequin Books S.A.

Printed in U.S.A.

Books by Karen Rose Smith

Silhouette Romance

Adam's Vow #1075
Always Daddy #1102
Shane's Bride #1128
†*Cowboy at the Wedding* #1171
†*Most Eligible Dad* #1174
†*A Groom and a Promise* #1181
The Dad Who Saved Christmas #1267
‡*Wealth, Power and a Proper Wife* #1320
‡ *Love, Honor and a Pregnant Bride* #1326
‡*Promises, Pumpkins and Prince Charming* #1332
The Night Before Baby #1348

Silhouette Special Edition

Abigail and Mistletoe #930
The Sheriff's Proposal #1074

*Darling Daddies
†The Best Men
‡ Do You Take This Stranger?

Previously published under the pseudonym Kari Sutherland

Silhouette Romance

Heartfire, Homefire #973

Silhouette Special Edition

Wish on the Moon #741

KAREN ROSE SMITH

lives in Pennsylvania but, after researching settings for
this book, has decided she'd like to visit Arizona in the
future. She insists one of the best aspects of writing
romances is learning new locations, though her favorite
part is writing the happily-ever-after. Readers can write
to her at P.O. Box 1545, Hanover, PA 17331.

Olivia McGovern and Lucas Hunter

are delighted to announce

their surprise marriage

and the upcoming birth of their

little corporate dividend.

Prologue

"Maybe you should return to the party before I do," Lucas Hunter suggested to Olivia as he buckled his belt. Still disconcerted by a passion he didn't understand, his tone was more brusque than he intended. His sudden, overwhelming desire for this woman had led him to invite her to the privacy of his office where they'd talked for a while then...

The awkwardness between them was as palpable as the silence as she buttoned her ivory silk blouse and straightened her skirt. Her green gaze met his for the first time since they'd made love on the black leather couch.

"We might avoid gossip if I go back first." Olivia's voice was still slightly husky with the breathlessness that had characterized their lovemaking.

Lovemaking. What a poor choice of words. Somehow the sparks he always felt whenever he passed Olivia McGovern in the halls of the Barrington Corporation had ignited tonight as they'd fallen into conversation at the office party, kissed under the mistletoe and gone to his office. Discovering that they were both spending Christmas Eve alone, they'd somehow found themselves in an embrace on the couch.

He'd only had one glass of spiked punch and couldn't blame it on that.

And to top things off, she'd been a virgin!

A virgin.

Totally unexpected. Especially since the rumors circulating about her and her boss, Stanley Whitcomb, seemed to be proven by the late nights Olivia spent in Stanley's office, their familiar rapport, her glances of admiration for the man when she thought no one was watching.

"Lucas…"

"Let's not try to explain this, Olivia. Blame it on the holiday. Blame it on palms swaying in December. Phoenix might not have snow, but it has its own Christmas charm. We simply succumbed to the season. I'm just sorry that… I mean, if you had told me it was your first time—"

Her face was flushed with embarrassment. "I never expected this to happen."

"Neither of us did." He knew better than to expect honesty from a woman, or innocence. But the vulnerability in Olivia's eyes told him she'd been just as surprised as he'd been by the tempestuous desire that had overtaken them.

He reminded himself that she was a paralegal, studying for the bar, with designs on her boss. After his last relationship, Lucas had no desire to trust in more from a woman than a few moments of pleasure. "Go on back to the party, Olivia. Nothing happened here that can't be forgotten."

She hesitated, then ran her fingers through her long auburn hair and unlocked the door. When she closed it behind her, he told himself he *could* forget.

And he would.

Christmas bells sounded outside. He took a deep breath, inhaling the lingering scent of Olivia's perfume, remembering her satin skin under his fingertips, the shuddering of his body as he'd made her his.

He *would* forget.

Because he'd never unlock his heart to a woman again.

Chapter One

Olivia rushed past the oleander hedges bordering the masonry wall at the side entrance to the Barrington Corporation. The scent of citrus seemed to trail after her in the early-February breeze, a fragrance she usually enjoyed. But for the past few weeks...

Now she knew why she couldn't keep her breakfast down, why she'd preferred only tea for lunch, why the "virus" that had begun soon after Christmas Eve had continued to plague her. Because it wasn't a virus.

As her doctor had told her during her lunch hour—she was pregnant.

Almost oblivious to the pleasant blue, tan and deep salmon accoutrements of the east wing of Barrington, a corporation that owned everything from vacation getaways in the States to hotels in Europe, she jabbed at the button for the third floor and the legal division. She'd planned her life and looked forward to becoming a full-fledged lawyer. She'd woven a dream about her and a stable man—her boss.

But now...what was she going to do?

If only she and Lucas Hunter hadn't kissed under the mistletoe, hadn't talked about being alone on Christmas Eve, hadn't bonded in some inexplicable way that night and ended up making love on the couch in his office!

It was behavior alien to her. It had been the first time she'd ever made love to a man, for goodness' sake. And the aftermath? They'd dressed, an awkward silence between them. And after a brief conversation that hadn't helped the awkwardness at all, they'd gone back to the party separately as if nothing had happened.

That one night, that indiscretion, that excitement she'd felt the first moment she'd seen Lucas Hunter when he'd come to work at Barrington six months ago, was going to change her life forever!

Her hand protectively fell across her stomach as she stepped onto the elevator and it rose to the third floor. She'd love this child no matter what happened. She'd—

When the elevator door slid open, Lucas stood there as sexy and rakishly handsome as ever. Her mouth went dry and her hands became clammy. He was wearing the same fine navy suit he'd worn on Christmas Eve. His tawny blond hair fell across his brow just as casually as when she'd run her fingers through it....

"Hello, Olivia."

Lucas's deep voice seemed to vibrate under her hand on her tummy, and she quickly dropped it to her side. The politeness in his blue eyes and their cool remoteness led her to compose herself as she stepped from the elevator. "Good afternoon, Lucas."

Straightening her shoulders, she forced herself to walk toward Stanley Whitcomb's office and forget for the moment Lucas was the father of her child. She had to sort her thoughts before she could decide what to do about this baby...and Lucas Hunter. When she should tell him. *If* she should tell him.

As she walked down the hall, she thought about the rumors she'd heard about Lucas. Opening the door to Stanley's office suite, she greeted Stanley's secretary, June, with the best smile she could muster and settled behind the teak desk. She'd worked here as a paralegal part-time as she finished law school but full-time since the end of summer when she'd missed the bar exam. In August she'd gone home to Tuscon for the test, prepared to pass and begin her future. But on the way to the exam she'd gotten tied up by a traffic accident! If an applicant was late for the two-day testing, even five minutes, he or she had to wait until the next time it was given and try again. *Nothing* would keep her from taking the exam at the end of February. This time it would be given in Phoenix, and she'd make absolutely sure she was there on time with plenty to spare.

The door to Stanley's office opened, and he brought a folder to her desk. As always, the touch of gray in his black hair added to his distinguished look. In his late forties, he was fit and trim. He'd been widowed for ten years and was everything stable she'd ever searched for in a man. Since she'd come to Barrington, he'd been her mentor, and all she'd wanted was for him to notice her as a woman rather than as his paralegal.

But now…

Stanley placed the folder on her desk. "Those are the new contracts for managers— Olivia, you're very pale. Are you feeling all right?"

Hormones must be addling her brain as well as her stomach. All she could think about was Lucas, Christmas Eve and the doctor's smile when he'd told her the baby would arrive at the end of September.

Suddenly the weight of all of it closed in on her. "Actually, I am feeling a little under the weather. Can I take those contracts home?" She'd never asked for time off before, except for the bar exam.

"Of course you can," Stanley said quickly. "Give me a call if you have any questions."

Her boss was such a nice man. Without Lucas's edge. Without the aura of restrained sensuality, without—

Standing, she gave Stanley a weak smile, picked up the folder and her purse and left the office.

Olivia intended to drive home, make herself a cup of tea and think. But as she passed a shopping mall and saw a children's store, she impulsively circled the block and found a spot in the parking lot near the shop. Impulsiveness had never been part of her nature. Since she was old enough to realize her dad's spontaneity and dream-chasing took him away from home and hurt her mother, she had vowed to be dependable and mature for her mom's sake. Maturity meant planning, taking responsibility, working toward a goal.

As she crossed the threshold of the store and found herself in the midst of cribs, mobiles, strollers and high chairs, she felt like Dorothy landing in Oz. She wandered past a row of car seats and into the section with clothes, stopping before a rack of baby shirts. They were so small! When she moved into the infant section, the enormity of being pregnant as well as being a mother seemed both glorious *and* totally overwhelming.

She closed her eyes for a moment and saw Lucas Hunter's face.

He had the right to know he was going to be a father.

Now.

Hurrying out of the store, she hoped Lucas hadn't been leaving to fly off somewhere. He'd been hired by Rex Barrington II to handle a sensitive merger negotiation, then he'd stayed on to handle another. The news that he owned his own plane and could fly anywhere Rex needed him to go at the drop of a hat had spread through the offices his first week at the complex. It was also well-known that he flew off somewhere almost every weekend. Personnel said he wasn't married.

But he could very well be *involved.* Olivia's heart raced at the thought of telling him her news.

Information concerning the hotel in Grand Junction, Colorado, that Barrington was thinking about acquiring should have filled Lucas's mind with facts and figures he usually analyzed like a human calculator. But ever since he'd run into Olivia at the elevator...

His descent into lunacy on Christmas Eve had haunted him for the past five weeks—as had Olivia's face, her smile, the wonder in her eyes.

The light knock on his office door was a welcome intrusion.

Since his stay at Barrington was temporary, he'd

insisted he didn't need a secretary. He flew to hotel locations or was involved in meetings as much as he worked in his office.

"Come in," he called, expecting a courier or Rex Barrington himself.

When Olivia opened the door, Lucas denied the fact that his blood was rushing faster. She looked pale but as lovely as always in an emerald green suit the same color as her eyes.

Before he could stand, she came inside, clenched her hands in front of her over her purse and said, "I'm pregnant."

All of his life, Lucas had learned that composure was the secret of handling others, to taking charge, to easing any complicated situation. "And what would you like me to do about it?" he asked calmly and evenly as if he were discussing a merger.

Her green eyes registered surprise...and then hurt. He didn't think he'd ever recognize hurt in a woman's eyes again without thinking she was trying to manipulate him. But before he could reassess his response and the best way to proceed, Olivia turned and fled his office.

Coming to his feet, Lucas started after her. As he glanced down the hall, he didn't see her at the elevator but he heard the thud of the stairwell door. How could she move so fast in those high heels?

Inside the stairwell, he caught a flash of green as she rounded the last flight. "Olivia. Wait!"

But either she didn't hear him or didn't care to hear him. Finally he caught up to her in the parking lot as she fumbled with her key to unlock her car door. When she ignored him, he clasped her elbow. "We need to talk."

She pulled her arm from his grasp. "I don't think so."

"Olivia, you took me by surprise."

Going still, she stared up at him. "I don't *expect* you to do anything about this. I just felt you had the right to know."

There was something he had to ask. "Are you sure this baby's mine?"

Where before he'd seen hurt in her eyes, now he saw anger. Inserting her key in the lock, she opened her door.

"Olivia..."

"I wouldn't have come to you if I weren't sure. I've never slept with another man, Lucas, so there's no doubt this baby is yours."

She slid into the driver's seat, but before she could close the door, he grabbed it. "We're going to discuss this. Either here, your place or mine. What's your preference?"

After a few defiant moments, she said, "I live about ten minutes from here."

"I'll follow you."

As Lucas drove away from Barrington, keeping Olivia's small blue car in sight, his mind spun.

Olivia was pregnant with his child.

She'd never slept with another man.

Over the past month, he'd noticed her spending more and more evenings with Stanley and thought for sure they'd become a couple.

What if she was lying to him? Celeste had lied to him for months, claiming to love him, swearing she'd love to have children. Until he'd finally taken her to his foster parents' ranch, told her about his background and witnessed firsthand that she didn't like children any more than she appreciated peanut butter and jelly sandwiches. She'd been attracted to his success as much as his elegant town house and small plane, and expected champagne and caviar in her future. Why hadn't he realized sooner she wasn't the type of woman who could cope with kids' messy fingers and skinned knees?

Because he'd wanted his own family too badly to see the truth.

After Celeste, he'd decided if he wanted a family, he could adopt a child on his own. But his desire for Olivia on Christmas Eve had shown him a woman could still arouse passion that he thought had died along with his involvement with Celeste.

Mim and Wyatt, his foster parents, had taught him well—about hard work and values and consequences. But this consequence was one he'd never expected. And he realized Olivia would have no reason to lie to him. If this child *were* Stanley Whitcomb's and she loved Whitcomb, she wouldn't look as if the bottom had dropped out of her world.

Following Olivia into northwest Phoenix, Lucas drove to a modest, green-landscaped apartment complex that was very different from the planned community in Scottsdale where his town house was located. He pulled into a guest space at the reserved parking area and climbed out of the car. They didn't speak as Olivia showed him to an inside corridor where they mounted a flight of stairs. As she let him into her apartment, he took a quick look around.

Olivia didn't live in luxury, but her small apartment felt much more homelike than his larger town house. Actually the sky-blue plaid sofa with its many pillows and colorful afghan thrown over its back, the unfinished pine tables and the braided rug gave him the same comfortable feeling as the living room at Mim and Wyatt's ranch. A white enamel table for two sat at the edge of the living room. Olivia's kitchen was so small, two people sharing its space would definitely bump shoulders and hips.

But his attention didn't stray long away from her pale face or her determined green eyes as she said, "I don't need your help and I don't want it."

The desire for Olivia he'd thought he could forget urged him closer to her. "If this is my child, too, I have rights."

"Rights won't make you a parent. Rights won't make you take responsibility. I know how men only assert their rights when it's convenient for them! And if you don't even believe this child is yours—"

He clasped her shoulders. "You've never slept with Stanley Whitcomb?"

As she went rigid under his hands, her gaze didn't waver from his. "No. I've never slept with Stanley or any other man. And if you don't believe me…"

Gut instinct along with logic told him she was being honest. "I believe you."

Suddenly, the family Lucas had always longed for seemed within his grasp. Wasn't he an expert at taking the unexpected and making it serve his purposes? He'd learned young to make the best of what he had, what he earned, what he took. And sometimes reaching out and taking got him exactly what he wanted.

When he bent to Olivia, she gave a small gasp. With the advantage of surprise on his side, his mouth came down on hers. He didn't want her to think, just to react, to give him a sign that the idea he'd grasped like an orphan searching for parents wasn't completely absurd. His tongue thrust into her mouth, look-ing for passion, asking if Christmas Eve had been an anomaly, praying a dream might be within his reach.

They fused into remembered intimacy for at least a hundred heartbeats, and then Olivia wrenched away.

She looked even more shaken than when she'd made her announcement. Wrapping her arms around herself, she asked, "Why did you do that?"

His composure back in place, his guard hiding the simmering desire, he answered her calmly. "To prove a point. There's fire between us, Olivia. We discov-ered it on Christmas Eve, and we've kept our distance from it since. I want you to consider marrying me."

"You *can't* be serious."

"I'm very serious. I was born a bastard. No child of mine will wear that label. I *will* be a father to this child. That's my undeniable right. And he or she will be as much *my* responsibility as yours."

Her hands fluttered between them. "Lucas, the idea is crazy. We don't even know each other."

"Believe me, I know that two parents are better than one, and that an alliance with that fire behind it has a better chance than any romantic illusion you might favor. Think about it."

Her complexion was pale again, and he realized that he'd better back off, not push, and let her con-sider what he'd said. Crossing to the door, he opened it. "Think about our child, Olivia. Try to put him or her first with any decision you make."

As Lucas stepped out into the hall, he realized his negotiating skills could help him seal the most critical merger of his life.

Sitting at the cream marble vanity in the lounging area of the ladies' room at Barrington the next morning, Olivia sipped from a mug of tea. She could have stayed in the break room for a few minutes, but she simply didn't feel like making conversation with friends when she was trying to decide the best course of action for her life...and her child's. Lucas's child.

The door to the ladies' room opened and Molly Doyle walked across the salmon carpeting to the wicker love seat nearest the vanity. "What's wrong, Olivia? You don't usually grab a cup of tea and run."

"It's just a busy morning."

With her straight blond hair flowing along her face, Molly tilted her head. "Busy or not, you used to devour cherry-cheese Danish with the rest of us. But lately..."

Molly was Olivia's closest friend at Barrington, and she knew she could trust her. She needed someone to confide in. Last night, she'd thought about calling her mother, but she wanted to have her life in better focus before she did. "I'm pregnant."

Molly didn't look surprised. "The way you turn green around food, I suspected you were. When are you and Stanley getting married?"

Not only Molly, but the four other women she usually shared lunch and breaks with, knew she hoped to marry her boss someday. Embarrassed and unnerved about what had happened at the company Christmas party, she'd told no one about it. "Lucas Hunter is the father."

Surprised, but recovering quickly, Molly said, "I heard a rumor that you and Lucas kissed under the mistletoe at the Christmas party. I thought whoever started it must have been mistaken." After a pensive pause, her friend asked, "What about Stanley?"

"I had hoped Stanley would see me as a woman and an equal after I pass the bar. I had hoped..." She trailed off, wondering why the lost hopes didn't disturb her as much as the desire in Lucas's eyes.

"Have you told Lucas?"

"Yesterday."

"And?" her friend prompted.

"He asked me to marry him, but I don't think he meant it. How could he? We don't know each other."

Molly's brows raised.

"It was only once," Olivia said in explanation.

"One time is all it takes. And as for Lucas not meaning his proposal, that doesn't sound like him. Lucas Hunter impresses me as a man who knows exactly what he's doing at all times. And from what I hear, Rex Barrington trusts him implicitly because of that. What did you answer when he proposed?"

"It wasn't a proposal exactly. More like an offer of a merger. And I didn't answer him. He told me to think about it."

"What do *you* want?"

She remembered Christmas Eve; she relived Lucas's kiss; she brought to mind words associated with Lucas Hunter, words like *stud* and *loner* and *master negotiator.* He could fly away at a moment's notice, and his stay at Barrington was rumored to be temporary. "I don't *know* what I want. I had my life planned." She took a deep breath and decided, "I have to think my way out of this."

Molly patted her arm. "This might not be as simple as solving a problem with logic or fine-tuning a contract. Don't forget to let yourself feel as well as think." After checking her watch, she frowned. "I've got to get back to advertising. I've been having trouble concentrating, and my work is backed up.''

"Jack?" Olivia asked, knowing Molly wished for more than a platonic friendship with *her* boss.

"I had a dream about him last night. And I find myself sitting at my desk daydreaming—" She stopped. "Are you sure you'll be all right?"

Olivia gave her friend a grateful smile. "I'll be fine. I just have to sort it all out. Thanks for listening."

"Anytime. You know that."

As Molly pulled open the door, Olivia stood. She took a deep breath and closed her eyes. Again Lucas's face appeared behind her eyelids, his blue gaze challenging her to find the right direction for not only herself, but for their child.

Knowing how to bide his time, when to sweeten the deal and when to stand on a firm line, Lucas carried a box filled with sandwiches and drinks into Whitcomb's office suite. June saw him first and smiled. Lucas gave a perfunctory nod and headed for Olivia's desk. When she looked up, he rested the box on the corner.

Stanley came out of his office. "Hi, Lucas. Do we have a meeting I've forgotten?"

"No. I came to take Olivia to the courtyard for lunch."

Stanley appeared as surprised as his secretary who quizzically glanced at Olivia. As did Lucas. The ball was in her court.

Her gaze locked to his, then shifted to Stanley. "Is it convenient for me to leave now?" she asked her boss.

"Sure. And don't worry about rushing back. You were in here working this morning before any of us."

When Lucas noticed Olivia's face flush slightly, he wondered if she always blushed when Whitcomb was close to her. If she was really in love with the man...

But Lucas knew marriage meant more than flowers and spinning dreams. He'd seen Mim and Wyatt weather the years. Marriage wasn't a fairy tale; it was hard work...with pleasure and good times thrown in, if you were lucky.

He had no doubt he and Olivia could find the pleasure again. Yesterday's kiss had proven that. Even now, there was a simmering tension zipping between them.

Olivia took her purse from her desk drawer and came around from behind her desk. "I'm ready."

Once they reached the hall, she said, "You could have warned me."

"I didn't want to give you a chance to refuse."

"If I truly didn't want to go to lunch with you, I would have refused anyway."

He chuckled and started walking. "I'll remember that next time."

After they took the elevator to the ground floor, Lucas avoided the cafeteria and went through a door that led outside. Round redwood tables and chairs were scattered across the flagstone patio. It was early and they were alone outside except for a group of employees he didn't know. Choosing a table secluded from the others by a potted palm, he set down the box and pulled out a chair for her. "Do you always come to work early?"

She sat and glanced over her shoulder at him. "I didn't sleep much last night." Her silky hair, full of waves that slid over her shoulder, glistened with red in the daylight.

"Thinking about the baby…or marriage?"

"Both." She turned back to the table, avoiding his gaze.

At least she hadn't dismissed the idea as ridiculous. He seated himself across from her and handed her a tuna sandwich with a carton of milk. "When do you take the bar?"

As she opened the sandwich wrapper, she leaned back. "The end of the month."

Taking a hefty bite of his sandwich, he watched her break off a piece of the white bread crust and pop it into her mouth. She looked a little pale again.

"It seems like forever until you take the bar and receive notification of whether you passed."

"You remember?" she asked with a smile.

Although he was thirty-four and nine years past the bar exam, he remembered the waiting well. "I had a lot riding on that notification. Several people had put their faith in my ability to succeed."

"Your family?"

"I don't have a family, Olivia." But he didn't want to go into that with her. Not now. Not yet. "Aren't you going to eat?"

She picked up the sandwich, but as she brought it to her mouth, she practically turned green. Abruptly setting it in front of her, she pushed it to his side of the table. "Lucas, I'm sorry. But the smell of tuna—"

Suddenly he understood and whisked it away from her and stood. "Are you sure it's just the tuna? Maybe you should go to a doctor."

"I was just at my doctor's yesterday. It's morning sickness, only I have it most of the day."

"You *have* to eat," he advised, a protective feeling he never experienced before engulfing him.

"I realize that. But some smells and tastes make it worse."

"What can I get you?"

"Lucas, really…"

"I'm going to buy you lunch. Would you like to go somewhere else?"

His determination must have convinced her. "A turkey sandwich would be fine. And a soda—without caffeine."

"Anything else?"

"No, thanks. The doctor told me eating a little bit more often would help."

"I'll be right back." He almost added, "So don't go running off." But Olivia didn't look as if she would run anywhere. She was still too pale.

As he set off for the cafeteria, he decided he needed to go to a bookstore and buy a few books on pregnant women. Information was power, and he needed some power where Olivia was concerned.

An almost balmy breeze lifted the strands of Olivia's hair. She let the peace and sunny weather soothe her as the nausea subsided. Lucas had looked so…puzzled as to what to do with her. She had to smile. She guessed he was used to being in charge and on top of every situation. Even on Christmas Eve as he'd admitted he was spending the night alone, there was a confidence about him that suggested if he *was* alone, it was by choice.

Would Christmas Eve ever have happened if she hadn't missed spending the holiday with her mother? But Rosemary McGovern had gone on a well-deserved vacation with a few other teachers and Olivia had encouraged her. Her mother had worked hard and sacrificed to put her daughter through law school, helping as much as she could.

Lucas had said he had no family. No connections? No bonds? Then where did he fly off to on weekends?

A few minutes later, she spotted Lucas as he pushed through the glass doors. He was so tall...so absolutely assured...so... The word that kept coming to mind was *sexy*. And that's the attribute that had gotten her into trouble in the first place. Not only the way he looked, but the way he touched and kissed.

This time he carried a tray with a turkey sandwich and a soda.

As he set it in front of her, she gazed up at him and couldn't look away. Why wouldn't her insides stop trembling whenever he came too close? Finally she managed to say, "Thank you."

When he was settled across from her again and had popped the top on his cola, he said, "You mentioned you'd been thinking about marriage."

It was a lead-in, meant to start a discussion. But she didn't really feel there was much to discuss. "I can't marry you, Lucas. You're...a...a...stranger!"

"Not quite," he countered in a rich, even tone that conveyed exactly what he was picturing.

Her pulse sped up and she took a small bite of her sandwich to give herself a few moments. "I won't compound one mistake by making another. We need more than..."

"*Desire* is the word, Olivia. And I'd say it's a good start. But maybe you're right. We don't have to rush. After all, we have another...what...eight months until the baby's born?"

"The end of September," she murmured, feeling uneasy, knowing by the look in his eyes that he was planning some strategy.

He gave her a slow smile. "If you won't marry me yet, will you come live with me?"

Chapter Two

"Just consider it a compatibility test," Lucas suggested with more levity than he felt.

"A compatibility test," Olivia repeated warily.

"Sure." He leaned forward and inhaled the tease of her perfume that could draw him even closer if the table weren't separating them. "Let's face it, Olivia. We have the chemical mix. If we have compatibility, too, what else do we need?"

Her furrowed brow told him she could give him a few answers to that question, but he was sure they'd have more to do with fantasy than reality. Covering her hand, he used persuasion for the skill it was. "This child deserves the best we can give him. Shouldn't we at least give living together a fair chance?"

As she still hesitated, he wondered if Stanley Whitcomb was the reason. "If you're worried about gossip, no one has to know. At least not yet. And until we see if we're compatible, our relationship can be strictly platonic.''

"We'd be roommates?"

"Exactly. The guest bedroom has a lock on the door, if that makes you feel better about the idea."

Pulling her hand away from his, she slid back on her chair. "I need to think about this, Lucas."

He realized he'd pushed as far as he could. Too much persuasion might make her feel coerced. "You don't usually act on impulse, do you?"

"No, I don't."

"What happened on Christmas Eve?"

Though her cheeks flushed, she didn't avoid his gaze. "I don't know. I've never done anything that impulsive in my life. I *always* look at the repercussions. I never intended to have sex before I was married. It was a vow I made to myself a long time ago."

Her answer surprised him. He didn't think women in this day and age believed in abstinence before marriage any more than men. "Why?"

"Because making love is important and special and should go along with commitment."

He couldn't decide whether Olivia was simply inexperienced or naive.

"You're looking at me as if I'm from another planet."

"I'm just wondering if you see the world the way it is or the way you want it to be," he concluded gruffly.

"Both."

"So you admit you're an idealist?"

"Oh, Lucas. If I don't have an ideal, what can I strive for?"

The way she said his name rippled through him in

a manner as arousing as her touch. The more he knew about her, the more desire flamed higher, unsettling him. "I strive for what's attainable. I know the difference between what I can grasp and what I can't. I know what's real. This baby and the desire between us are real." After a pause when he knew they were both thinking about the reality of becoming parents, he pulled another tool from his repertoire. When negotiations stall, make a reasonable request. "Why don't you come over to my place after work? Look around. See if you'd be comfortable there."

She studied him for a long moment, and he wished he could read her mind.

"All right," she said softly. "I'll come over after work. To look."

He might be a master negotiator, but he had the feeling that Olivia would only do what was right for her, no matter how skillful he was at persuasion.

As Olivia followed the directions Lucas had given her through Scottsdale, she passed hotels, resorts and streets lined with boutiques, galleries and restaurants. Even at dusk, she was amazed at how green the landscape appeared here, although the city sat in the middle of the Sonoran Desert. Golf courses abounded along with several parks. She headed north toward the McDowell Mountains and as darkness suddenly wrapped around her, she easily found the planned neighborhood where Lucas lived.

Stopping at the gatehouse of Desert Vista, she gave her name. The security guard motioned her toward multilevel residences. Red-tile roofs glowed under the lighting that was subtle rather than intrusive. The white exteriors took on a mellow glow as palm trees as well as pines sheltered curving pathways leading to Mediterranean-style buildings. After she parked where Lucas had suggested, she walked beneath private terraces and under an arch that led into a courtyard. Finding his town house number, she climbed the steps and rang the bell.

He opened the door to her. "C'mon in."

She'd never seen him in casual clothes. He was wearing an off-white knit shirt and khaki slacks. His moccasins and lack of socks added to his relaxed appearance. The excitement she always felt when she looked at him seemed heightened by the fact that she was crossing the threshold into his home.

The vaulted ceiling with its fan drew her attention to a two-bedroom loft. As she pulled her gaze from the upstairs and thoughts of what could happen there, she concentrated on the adobe fireplace, a long contemporary sofa upholstered in earth tones and spruce, a complementary high-armed, oversize, almost square chair. The distressed pine coffee table, entertainment center and occasional tables accented the elegant but relaxed decor.

"I'll give you a tour," he offered, his smile making her stomach flip-flop. As he led her through the dining room with its Santa Fe-style hutch and table for four, she wondered if he entertained often.

"You have a beautiful place," she commented when she entered the kitchen with its black appliances and eat-in counter.

"Wait until you see the view," he said with a conspiratorial wink. Sliding doors led from the kitchen onto the covered terrace.

An almost full moon glowed over blue-black mountain tops, and cascades of stars decorated the sky. The temperature was dropping, but she hardly noticed with Lucas standing so close to her, his arm almost grazing hers.

"There's a pool and clubhouse with a weight room. And maid service."

As she took it all in, doubts still plagued her. "As I said, Lucas, it's beautiful here. But a pretty view and nice furniture won't convince me to move in with you."

"What will?" he asked, his deep voice intent on convincing her, no matter what it took.

"I don't know. I have to think about it more."

"You didn't see the guest room."

"I don't *have* to see the guest room to know I could live here comfortably." Matter of fact, going anywhere near that loft with Lucas could give her even more doubts.

"What's the problem, Olivia?" he asked, turning and stepping closer.

"I...I have to make sure moving in would be the best decision."

"How will you know unless you try it?"

She touched her heart with her fingers. "It has to feel right in here."

When he reached out, she started to tremble. And as his hand caressed her face...

"Don't." She pulled away, shaken.

"You didn't seem to find my touch repulsive on Christmas Eve." There was anger edging the frustration in his voice.

"Oh, Lucas. I need to think clearly, and I can't when we're too...close."

"Is it Whitcomb?" he asked gruffly.

All of her feelings and thoughts were confused

right now. Her life had taken a direction she'd never expected. For the last few months she'd envisioned Stanley in her future. And now...

"It's my whole future, Lucas. And yours. And the baby's. Aren't you confused? Don't you feel off balance, like you've been thrown the biggest curve of your life?"

In the shadows of the moon and the kitchen light, his brow creased. "I've had lots of curves. This time I know what I want."

"Well, I don't. And I won't let you push me when I'm not sure. I don't want to be food for the whispering grapevine. Yet I don't like secrecy or deception, either. I've only known about this baby for two days—" Tears came to her eyes and she blinked them away. She *never* cried, and she wouldn't let Lucas Hunter see her doing it now.

His composure slipped and he grabbed her shoulders. "You're not thinking of ending the pregnancy?"

The searing heat of his hands warned her about the passion that had been a stranger to her until Christmas Eve. Even now, she didn't know it or understand its depth. "Of course not. I would *never* consider not keeping this child."

He looked relieved, then released her. "If you need time to think...think. But as this baby's father, Olivia, I won't let you put me off or brush me aside. Understand?"

It was as if fatherhood were a crusade for Lucas. Was he so vehement because of a well-honed sense of responsibility? She remembered his words. *I was born a bastard.* Had he never known a father? She needed some breathing space to think about it...to think about him and what living here could mean.

She replied, "I do understand, Lucas, but I won't rush into anything, certainly not living with you." Then she turned away from him and his compelling presence, as well as away from the temptation to see him as more than her baby's father.

As Olivia went grocery shopping on Saturday, she stopped in the baby food aisle and studied the different brands, then passed the toothbrushes, imagining hers hanging next to Lucas's. Her mind spun with thoughts—some pleasant, some overwhelming, some downright frightening. Was she equipped to be a good mother? Did she want to raise a child alone? Could she imagine being a partner to Lucas? Being more?

The questions raced through her mind all day Saturday, causing another sleepless night through which she prayed for guidance. Going to church on Sunday morning, she asked for a sign and realized she was being foolish. She had gotten herself into this predicament; she couldn't expect divine intervention to get her out.

As she prepared herself a late breakfast of pancakes that she suddenly craved, the phone rang. Holding the receiver at her ear while she flipped a cake in the frying pan, she answered, "Hello."

"Baby. How are you?"

"Dad?" She hadn't heard from her father since last summer. At Christmas she'd hoped he'd call. More than that, she'd hoped he'd spend Christmas with her since her mother had been away. But he hadn't done either. "Where are you?" she asked as she switched off the burner.

"L.A. I'm working on a mail-order deal with a company that makes computer supplies. It's going great. If this goes through, I'll be a millionaire before I'm fifty-five!"

That was one of her dad's favorite lines. Only the age changed. The first time she'd heard it he'd told her he was was going to be a millionaire by age forty-five. She didn't think he'd ever kept a job longer than a few months. He preferred being an "independent contractor." That meant he was trying to sell something to someone. But he usually didn't call unless there was a problem.

"Are you really okay?"

There was a pause. "I'm fine. Now tell me what you've been doing. Are you a lawyer yet?"

"Come May, I hope." That was when she'd receive notification of whether or not she'd passed the bar. It was on the tip of her tongue to reveal she was pregnant. She'd always wanted to pour her heart out to her father, but he moved through life so quickly, she usually didn't get the chance. "Dad...I..."

"I called your mother. Invited her out here to go to Disneyland with me."

"What did she say?"

"That she has responsibilities and can't just take off for a week because I want her to. *You* know. The old story. I told her if she had spare investment capital, she could get in on the ground floor of this deal, but she wasn't interested in that, either."

"Now that I'm through school, Mom's saving for retirement."

"She wouldn't have to worry about retirement if she invested with me."

Nothing ever changed. Her father was still too self-absorbed to be concerned with anyone's life but his own.

"Matter of fact, if *you* want to invest—"

So *that's* why he'd called. Because of the deal. "Dad, I'm paying back loans."

"Sorry I can't help with that," he mumbled. "But in a year or so, I'll be sitting pretty and can pay for anything you need."

"I don't need anything, Dad."

After a few moments, he said, "Well, you *could* encourage your mother to give my new venture a chance—"

"Dad, Mom knows what she wants to do." And putting money into another of her ex-husband's pipe dreams wasn't it.

"Maybe, if you push it a little, she might reconsider."

When Olivia kept silent, feeling as if he'd called to use her rather than to ask about her life, he finally mumbled, "I gotta get going."

Still wanting contact with him, she said, "If you give me your address—"

"That will be changing soon. When I move to a bigger place, I'll give you a call. You take care, baby."

When she hung up, she had a hollow feeling inside. The same feeling she always had after she talked to her dad.

Unbidden, Lucas's words sounded in her ears. *I will be a father to this child. And he or she will be as much my responsibility as yours.*

Her father had never taken responsibility for his marriage or for his family. *Would* Lucas? What kind of man *was* Lucas Hunter? What kind of father would he be? She had to find out before she let him into her life, into her child's life. What better way to get to know him than to live with him?

He'd said it would be a compatibility test. It would be more than that—she'd discover whether she could trust him and depend on him to *be* a parent. Because if she couldn't, she would raise this child alone.

When Lucas returned from Flagstaff Sunday evening, he was smiling. Spending the weekend at the ranch with Mim, Wyatt and the four boys now under their care always refreshed him. And it wasn't the difference in temperature or altitude. Those boys looked up to him, and he felt ten feet tall acting as their big brother. After he dropped his duffel bag by the stairway, he saw the blinking light on his answering machine and pushed the button.

"Lucas. It's Olivia. Please call me when you get in."

It took him a matter of seconds to punch in her number. When she answered, he asked, "Is something wrong?"

"No. I thought about what we discussed. Moving in with you for a few weeks would be a good idea."

"For a few weeks?"

"Can we just take each day as it comes? We do need to get to know each other better. For the baby's sake."

He realized she was still uncertain about it, and he had to tread carefully. "We'll take one sunrise at a time. Would you like to come over now?"

"I did get some things together. But if you just got in…"

"C'mon over. We'll get you settled."

Lucas couldn't believe the anticipation he felt as he paced his living room for a while, then finally went outside. He didn't want Olivia carrying a heavy suitcase.

The temperature had dropped into the fifties. In a few weeks, spring would bloom here. But not in Flagstaff—that would take longer. There was snow frosting the ground there. He'd flown out before a front moved in that was supposed to bring more snow.

He'd walked the perimeter of the parking area when he spotted Olivia's car. As she pulled into one of the guest spaces, he met her at her door. A few minutes later, he carried her garment bag and suitcase up the stairs as she followed with a cosmetics case into the spare room.

"This is a lovely room," she said softly as she set the case on the mission-style dresser.

An interior decorator had furnished his town house. The guest bedroom with its cream and blue spread and drapes had never been slept in.

"If you need anything, just let me know. There's a master bath up here, a half bath downstairs. The blue towels are yours." He opened the bifold doors of her closet and hung the garment bag inside.

"Lucas, I'd rather not tell anyone yet about the pregnancy or me living here." After she shrugged off her sweater coat, she laid it across the bedroom chair.

His gaze locked to hers. "All right. But I'm not ashamed you're carrying my baby. Eventually everyone will know."

"Eventually." She laid her hand protectively over her stomach.

In jeans and a soft white sweater, Olivia looked lovely. Her auburn hair framed her face in gentle waves he'd love to run his fingers through. But he was afraid she'd bolt like a frightened colt. She was so slender that as soon as the baby started growing, everyone would know she was pregnant whether she wanted them to or not.

"What time do you usually turn in?" he asked.

"Earlier lately. Around ten. But if you don't mind, I think I'll take a bath, then go to bed."

"I'll be working downstairs for a while." Crossing to the door, he stopped. "This might seem awkward now. But we'll get used to living together."

When she gave him an uncertain smile, he closed her door...before he kissed her.

Olivia awakened at 2:00 a.m. craving something to eat. She didn't know why she woke up in the middle of the night, hungrier than she'd been all day. But when she did, she gave in and ate, knowing her body was telling her both she and the baby needed sustenance. Pulling on her white-and-green flowered satin robe, she opened the door and saw a small lamp glowing in the living room.

Glancing across the loft, she noticed Lucas's door was closed. But it had been closed earlier, too. The bare wood floor was cool under her feet as she went down the steps, through the living room and into the kitchen. Lucas was sitting at the counter, still dressed, a laptop computer open in front of him. Just looking at his broad shoulders, the back of his neck and his tawny blond hair gave her insides a funny little lurch.

"I'm surprised you don't have an office here," she said softly.

He glanced at her over his shoulder. "The long and short of it is that I don't spend much time here. I can take the laptop with me wherever I go and have everything I need.''

One thing Olivia had noticed about Lucas's home was that it didn't look lived-in. No papers or magazines lying around—no clutter. She always left a tea mug sitting somewhere, or notes from work. And knickknacks that brought back memories were very important to her. Lucas's table surfaces were clear except for a carefully chosen sculpture or a lamp.

''You travel a lot, don't you?'' Maybe she could find out where he went on weekends.

Swiveling around on the rattan-backed wooden stool, he shrugged. ''I travel. But mostly when I work, I do it in my office. I've spent lots of nights on the couch there.''

The couch. Soft, supple leather. She could still remember the feel of it against her bare back, the exciting weight of Lucas on top of her....

His gaze dipped to her satin chemise-gown under her robe, the belt at her waist, her bare legs. The robe and gown suddenly felt very short...very revealing. When he stood, she thought about scurrying back to her room, but she knew if they were going to be housemates, she couldn't feel self-conscious every time he looked at her.

With her cheeks hot, she did move away from him toward the refrigerator. ''I didn't mean to bother you. I got hungry, and since that's a rare occasion these days, I thought it would be good to take advantage of it. Mind if I rummage around your refrigerator?''

''I don't mind. But you're not going to find much. I eat a lot of takeout.''

Opening the door, she found a half-dozen eggs and a stick of margarine in the door. Two cans of beer, a bottle of juice, a wedge of cheese and two cartons of leftover Chinese takeout sat on the top shelf.

"How hungry are you?" he asked. "I can make an omelet. Supper was a long time ago."

She wondered where he'd eaten and who he'd eaten with. "Sounds good," she murmured.

In a matter of minutes, Lucas had pulled a frying pan from a lower cabinet and set margarine melting in it. As he cracked an egg with one hand, he nodded to the cupboards along the side of the kitchen. "There's a box of crackers up there if you're interested."

The way her stomach was rumbling, she was definitely interested. She had to stretch on tiptoe to reach the top shelf. As she did, she felt Lucas's gaze on her. Her nightgown and robe had hiked up her thigh. Quickly she grabbed the box, and he looked away.

By the time Olivia had poured juice into two glasses and set their places, Lucas put two dishes on the counter. The eggs were done just right with cheese oozing from between the layers.

"I'll let you make me breakfast anytime," she teased, trying to establish a friendly rapport rather than a tingling one between them.

"I like to cook. I just don't do it very often." As he sat beside her, his leg grazed hers, his body heat tangible and tempting.

"Where did you learn?" she asked.

"Here and there."

She took a bite of the omelet, then set down her fork and studied him.

"What?" he asked.

"You're a lawyer through and through, aren't you?"

"What do you mean?"

"When I ask you a question, you don't really give me an answer. Is that design or habit?"

His blue eyes sparked with silver for a moment, and his silence told her he didn't like her observation. "Habit."

"Why?"

"Do you always ask so many questions?" he growled.

"I'm a lawyer, too."

"Not quite yet."

"You're changing the subject," she scolded.

After a quick glance at her, he replied, "I don't like talking about myself."

Olivia absorbed that as he quickly finished his omelet. With a few swallows he downed his juice and took his plate and glass to the sink.

Then he faced her again. "I'll be leaving early tomorrow morning. I have an appointment in Santa Fe." Opening a drawer, he took out a key and placed it on the counter. "You'll need that."

She nodded, thought about keeping silent and decided against it. "Lucas, I moved in here to get to know you better."

"And?" he prompted her.

"I can't do that if you won't let me."

He frowned. "I don't let people close easily, Olivia."

"And if I ask why, you won't tell me, will you?"

His brow creased and his eyes became a deeper blue. "How would you feel if I asked you for your life history in a nutshell?"

Another lawyer's tactic—answer a question with a question. "I might try and give it to you."

Her answer seemed to surprise him, but he responded, "What matters is who and what we are now."

"I don't *know* who you are."

Crossing to her, he stood very close. "I think you do or you wouldn't have moved in with me." The nerve in his jaw worked, and she knew if she tipped up her chin, he might kiss her. But she sat perfectly still.

He let out a breath. "It's late, Olivia. Finish up and get to bed. You need your sleep. I'll see you tomorrow."

Yes, she needed sleep. But she needed to get to know Lucas more. As he left the kitchen, she realized he was skilled at controlling a situation. She'd bide her time, then she'd show him he couldn't evade her questions so easily—not if he wanted to be a father to their child.

After Olivia bid Stanley and June good-night Monday evening, she walked down the hall to see if Lucas had returned yet from Santa Fe. His office door was locked. Disappointed, she crossed to the elevator, wondering if he might stay out of town overnight. Maybe there'd be a message waiting for her at the town house.

When the elevator dinged and the doors opened, five women exited and gathered around her with greetings and, "We're glad we caught you." She gave them all a wide smile. Molly, Sophia, Cindy and Rachel had invited her to lunch with them on her first day at Barrington. When she'd walked into the cafeteria not knowing anyone, ready to sit alone, they'd motioned her to their table.

She liked them all so much—Molly, whose hazel eyes were serious much of the time and who had become a trusted friend; Sophia, with her quick quips and easy laughter; Rachel, who'd had had a difficult time recovering from her last relationship, and Cindy, who had recently gotten engaged to Kyle Prentice, her boss. The fifth woman, Patricia, was Olivia's most recent friend at Barrington. All of them had gotten to know the pretty assistant personnel director better over the past month.

Sophia's curly blond hair bobbed as she hooked her arm through Olivia's. "Are you mad at us?"

"Mad? No, why?"

Patricia tilted her head and gazed at her with sparkling light green eyes. "Because you've been keeping to yourself lately. We never see you in the break room anymore."

"And rarely at lunch," Rachel added.

"Or are you having lunches with Stanley?" Cindy asked with a sly smile.

Molly kept silent.

"I've just been busy," Olivia answered, wanting to be honest but not quite yet ready to explain what was happening in her life.

"All the more reason to come out with us for supper. We haven't dished for ages," Cindy added.

Olivia *had* missed them all.

"For instance, did you know that Rex Barrington the Third fired his assistant?" Patricia asked. "She never even *saw* the man. And that was the problem. I made a mistake when I recommended her. I thought she'd be a self-starter and not need supervision. But I was wrong. Now I have to choose a replacement from the secretarial pool and hope I don't make another mistake.''

Rex Michael Barrington II would be retiring soon. Everyone expected his son, Rex III, to fill his shoes. But no one had ever seen Rex III. He was an elusive presence on the phone, giving orders, slowly taking over the reins of Barrington, yet never physically present. Rumors were that he was living in Europe and would only return after his father actually retired.

Sophia nudged Patricia. ''I'm in the running, aren't I? I've dreamed about being his new assistant.''

''You're definitely in the running,'' Patricia revealed with a smile.

''I'd like to come with you....'' Olivia began.

''Then do, Olivia. It will be good for you,'' Molly advised.

She couldn't tell them she had to make a phone call to leave a message because they'd have a million questions. They knew she didn't report to anyone. Maybe she could slip away and call from the restaurant in case Lucas returned to the town house before she did.

''All right. I'll come,'' she decided. ''And you can all catch me up on what you've been doing.''

''We all can imagine what Cindy's been doing,'' Sophia teased, as she pressed the button to open the elevator's doors.

Cindy just laughed.

Olivia stepped into the elevator with them, enjoying the conversation that buzzed around her, but also hoping she'd see Lucas later tonight.

Three hours later, Olivia parked behind Lucas's town house, hurried through the courtyard and up the steps. Time had flown, and it had been impossible for her to slip away to make a call. Even when she went to the ladies' room, one of her friends had joined her. Midway through dinner, relaxing as she hadn't for a while, and enjoying herself, she'd decided to stop worrying about calling. Lucas might even still be in Santa Fe.

Taking out the key he'd given her, tired from the long day, she found the door unlocked. As soon as she stepped into the ceramic entryway, Lucas came into the living room, white shirtsleeves rolled to the elbows, tie askew, his hair disheveled.

"Where in the blue blazes have you been?" he erupted.

She set her purse on the end table and unbuttoned her suit jacket. "Some friends and I went out."

"Drinking?" he asked with a restrained edge to his tone that told her he was angry.

"No! For supper."

"And you couldn't call and leave a message?"

"They caught me on my way out and I couldn't call without everyone asking questions. Why are you so upset?"

"I'm *not* upset."

Crossing to him, she said, "You *look* upset."

Ignoring that, he snapped, "If we're going to live together, Olivia, I expect the courtesy of a call if you're going to be late."

"Do the same rules apply to you?" She was getting annoyed that he had expectations she knew nothing about.

"*I'm* not pregnant."

His words hung in the air until the emotions inside her spurted out. "Well, it's a good thing, isn't it?

Because then maybe you couldn't fly off to one city after another, or work twenty hours a day or eat for the pleasure of it.'' She shook her head. ''I don't know what the rules are here, Lucas. You seem to have set some but didn't tell *me*.''

''There *are* no rules,'' he growled. ''If you'd just use your common sense—''

''My common sense told me I didn't want to make explanations to my friends about a situation that's... unsettled. My common sense told me you might stay in Santa Fe overnight. And my common sense is telling me, if you have expectations, I need to know what they are. But right now I'm beat and I'm going to bed.''

When she headed for the steps, he didn't move and he didn't speak. Halfway up, her conscience nudged her and she turned to face him. ''Lucas, I'm sorry if I worried you. I'll try not to let it happen again.''

She waited a moment, but he remained silent. The fatigue she'd been fighting throughout the evening engulfed her all at once. Turning, she climbed the rest of the stairs, wondering if Lucas always denied his feelings—and if he did, why?

Chapter Three

When Lucas hung up the phone in his office after a call from Rex Barrington's secretary, he checked his watch. Mildred Van Hess had confirmed his appointment with her boss for four o'clock. Chances were he'd be tied up until six. All day he'd had trouble concentrating, thinking about Olivia. He'd flown back from Santa Fe yesterday, expecting to have dinner with her—take her out someplace nice to make sure she ate. But he'd come home to an empty house, and as the minutes had passed, he'd called her office and then her apartment—with no luck.

He'd been worried about her, so much so that when she'd come home, he'd exploded! A strange reaction for a man who was always in control. But he'd never lived with a woman before. Asking Olivia to move in had been gut instinct, and he'd never expected it to be so difficult to stay away from her, not to push her, to deny the desire for her that was constantly with him. He'd left for work early this morning, before she was up, so he didn't *have* to deal with it. But now he realized that avoiding her was not a solution, and not what he wanted at all.

Picking up the phone, he dialed Olivia's extension. She picked up immediately.

"Olivia, it's Lucas."

There was only a brief pause. "Hello, Lucas."

As always, her soft tone made his heart beat faster. "I have a meeting with Rex that will probably keep me tied up until six or later. We could go out to eat after I get home."

"I was going to stop for groceries and make something." Her voice had lowered, probably so June couldn't hear at her desk across the office.

"I don't want you lifting lots of heavy bags," he decided.

"Just a few things for supper. Or would you really rather go out?"

He was surprised there was no rancor or bite to her voice as a residue from last night. Anytime he and Celeste had a skirmish, she'd pout for a week afterward. "Staying in tonight would be great. But I don't want you to go to a lot of trouble."

"No trouble, Lucas. I have to eat, too."

Clearly he owed her an apology, but he couldn't give it to her over the phone. "I'll see you tonight."

"Tonight," she repeated.

After Lucas hung up, he realized she hadn't given up on their compatibility test. Maybe tonight they could find common ground and build on it.

Lucas's entertainment center was high-tech, but Olivia finally figured out how to play one of her favorite CD's on it. By the time she'd browned chicken and set it simmering, she'd learned her way around the kitchen. When the phone rang, she picked it up without thinking and said hello.

"Oh! I must have dialed the wrong number," the woman at the end of the line said.

"Who are you trying to reach?"

"Lucas Hunter."

"He's not here right now, but I can give him a message."

After a brief silence the woman replied, "Just tell him to call the ranch."

"I'll do that." When Olivia hung up, she wished she had gotten a name. But the caller didn't seem to think it was necessary.

Supper began to disintegrate as seven came and went. Olivia ate alone at the dining room table, then made up a plate for Lucas and refrigerated it. When the door opened at eight-thirty and he walked in, his suit coat tossed over the crook of his arm, she woke. She'd dozed off on the sofa, a folder of contracts in her lap.

He dropped his briefcase on the chair with his jacket. "The discussion got complicated. I didn't mean to stand you up. I hope you ate."

"I did. And I made you a plate. But you probably sent out—"

"No, we didn't take the time. I would have called again if we'd taken a break."

She slid her feet to the floor. "Mr. Barrington has the reputation for always providing dinner when he takes a meeting late."

"He invited us out afterward."

"You turned down Rex Michael Barrington II's invitation to dinner?" she asked, knowing it was an honor the head of Barrington didn't extend to just any employee.

"I wanted to get home." Lucas came over and lowered himself beside her. "Olivia, I'm sorry about last night. I overreacted."

After thinking about it, she'd decided she was as much to blame as he was. "I should have called."

"I understand why you didn't. We don't have any ground rules. And the truth is—I've never lived with a woman before, and I'm not sure how to go about it."

For some reason that news filled her with satisfaction and a bit of wonder. "You haven't?"

He shook his head and reached out, stroking her cheek. "I can't stop thinking about Christmas Eve, Olivia, and considering the result, I'm feeling a little…off base."

The touch of his fingers against her skin made her tremble, but she managed to say, "You're not quite so intimidating when you're not so self-assured."

"You find me intimidating?" he asked with a smile.

"You have a reputation for being powerful and skillful and an expert at everything you do."

"Everything?" he repeated with glimmers of desire in his eyes hypnotizing her.

"Everything," she murmured on a breathless whisper as his head bent and his lips hovered close to hers.

"I don't want to intimidate you, Olivia," he said in a husky rasp. "I want to kiss you."

Excitement and anticipation made speaking impossible. She tilted her chin up until her lips met his, and he knew she wanted the kiss, too.

His arm enveloped her, his hand burrowing under

her hair. When his lips invited her to a deeper knowing, when his tongue coaxed the seam of her lips apart, she knew exploring could lead her into deep, deep trouble. But Lucas didn't give her a chance to analyze, let alone think. His erotic assault whirled her senses like sand in the wind. As on Christmas Eve, she felt his need urge her to respond with hers.

As his musky scent, his forbidden taste, the wonderful strength of him swept her away, her hand slid up his arm to his shoulder and felt the heat of his skin through his shirt. When he thrust into her mouth again in response, she shivered with the arousal and pleasure she'd only known since Lucas. Tonight, as on Christmas Eve, his desire asked rather than took, and intrigued her into wanting more. The intensity of each stroke of his tongue, each press of his lips, encouraged her to know him this way, if no other.

Know him.

But she didn't know him. Not yet. And if she didn't pull back...

Her hand slipped from his shoulder to his chest, and she braced herself as she broke away.

"I said we'd keep this platonic, didn't I?" he asked in a voice as sexy as the desire still sparkling in his eyes.

"We have to." She slid away from him and stood.

"What if we can't?"

Never before had she felt such an extraordinary pull toward a man. She remembered dates in college that had gotten too hot, men who'd expected more than a kiss from her after they'd paid for dinner. She'd stopped then and she was stopping now before she stumbled into another situation like Christmas Eve.

"I won't let desire run my life, Lucas. I have too much at stake."

"And you think I don't?"

"I haven't met a man yet except for Stanley who didn't want—" When Lucas scowled, she stopped.

"If you want me to stay away from you, I'll stay away," he said angrily as he stood.

"Lucas…"

But he'd already headed for the kitchen.

With a sigh, she told herself she should have been more tactful. She told herself she never should have succumbed to his touch or his kiss. But it was too late for regrets.

This time Olivia felt retreat was much more advisable than discussion. Apparently Lucas was frustrated with her, but she had to be honest with him and herself. If she made love with him again, it wouldn't be in haste, without thought, with no regard for the consequences. She'd have to be *sure*.

After a long shower where the remembrance of his kiss hung around her as tangibly as the steam from the hot water, she settled in her bedroom chair with the folder of contracts. But she heard Lucas climb the stairs and go into his room. His door closed with a click. She had difficulty concentrating, and when her mind wandered to their conversation downstairs and his admission that he'd never lived with a woman, she suddenly remembered the phone call he'd received.

The caller hadn't said it was important, but there was no way to know. She had to tell him about it.

Slipping on her robe, she wished she had another that was longer and heavier. She thought briefly about getting dressed but decided that would be ridiculous.

Her pulse skipping faster, she went into the hall, then knocked on his door.

When he opened it, her breath caught. He was wearing black silk sleeping shorts and nothing else.

She couldn't seem to direct her eyes away from the curling light brown hair on his chest. But finally she raised her gaze to his and found a wary expression on his face. "I...uh...forgot to tell you something."

He stood silent and sensually imposing—all that tanned skin, his dark nipples, the whorl of hair descending beneath the band of his shorts...

Forcing herself to concentrate on her purpose for standing at his door, she managed to say, "A phone call came in for you. It was a woman. She didn't leave her name but said you should call the ranch."

"I'll take care of it." His voice was even and short as if she'd disturbed him.

"Lucas..."

"I have a phone call to make, Olivia. Next time just post the message on the refrigerator."

There was really nothing else to say to him right now, and it was obvious he didn't want to talk to her. She returned to her room, wondering why she felt so sad, wondering why she felt like crying.

Alone in the office suite, Olivia gathered the notes she'd made all morning and took them to Stanley's desk. Both he and June had left for lunch. When she was on the way back to her chair, Molly came into the office. "Are you ready for lunch?"

Olivia shook her head and felt light-headed. The nausea had been worse than usual this morning. Even the thought of food... "No. But thanks for asking."

"Olivia, you look really pale. Is there anything I can do? Bring you a soda?"

Olivia shook her head again and bent to the bottom desk drawer to file a paper. "I didn't sleep much last night."

"You need to take care of yourself. Why don't I come over and fix supper for us?"

Molly was a good friend and Olivia knew she would be discreet. Standing quickly, she moved toward the door to close it. She must have straightened up too fast because her head began to swim. Taking a deep breath, she said, "I moved in with Lucas."

"Moved in?"

"It's a compatibility test. We…" Her ears began ringing and little black dots appeared in front of her eyes. "We—" She grabbed her desk as the world tilted.

"Olivia!" Molly wrapped her arm around her waist and snagged the chair with her foot. When Olivia sat, she ducked her head between her legs.

"I'm calling Lucas," her friend decided.

"No!" Lucas had left again this morning before she'd awakened. She had no idea whether he was in or out of his office, or whether he'd want to be called.

But Molly had already moved to the phone. As she pressed in the numbers, she scolded, "You need to go home, get your feet up and relax." After a pause, she said, "Mr. Hunter, this is Molly Doyle. I'm with Olivia and she's not feeling well—we're in Mr. Whitcomb's office."

Olivia tried to raise her head, but as she did, the dizziness engulfed her again.

A few minutes later, the door opened and Lucas

strode in. She could only see his feet, but she could tell they *were* his feet.

"What's wrong?"

Turning her head carefully, she answered, "I'm just a little dizzy."

"I'm taking you to your doctor."

"No, you aren't. It will pass. I didn't have breakfast."

He crouched down beside her. "Or lunch?"

"Lucas, I just couldn't," she said to the floor because every time she moved, her head spun.

"Can you get me a cold, wet cloth?"

Olivia supposed he was talking to Molly because her friend left.

His arm came around her. It was so sturdy, the feel of his body so strong, she stopped struggling against the wave of dizziness, and sweat broke out on her forehead. Air cooled her as he lifted her hair. When Molly returned, Olivia suddenly felt the cloth on the back of her neck. In a few minutes, the black fuzziness passed and her ears stopped ringing.

When she raised her head, Lucas's face was very close to hers. "Better?" he asked.

She nodded.

Standing, he removed the cloth. His gaze on Molly, he asked, "Will you tell Mr. Whitcomb I took Olivia home?"

"Lucas, I'm fine now."

"You're as white as a sheet and you need something to eat. If you won't go to the doctor, I'm taking you home."

His authoritative tone annoyed her, and she stood to confront him toe-to-toe. But she swayed and suddenly found herself scooped up in his arms with no place to put hers but around his neck.

"The doctor's or home?" he growled.

"Home. But you're not going to carry me out of this building."

"Watch me. We'll take the stairs."

With a smile, Molly handed Olivia her purse.

"You're aiding and abetting," Olivia grumbled.

"For a good cause," Molly replied.

Lucas checked the hall before he carried her out the door, then descended the flights of stairs with her as if she were no heavier than his briefcase. At the outside door, she protested. "Put me down, Lucas. Let me get my sea legs." When he frowned, she asked, "Please?"

"If you're wobbly…"

"I'll hold on to your arm. Promise."

Setting her on her feet, he watched her carefully as he pushed open the door.

Olivia preceded him outside, aware of his gaze on her. She had a headache and felt exhausted, but not dizzy. As Lucas walked beside her, she felt his stability and his strength.

Lucas drove a top-of-the-line Jeep with a plush interior and a CD player. As they rode home in silence, Olivia rested her head against the seat. When he switched on the stereo system, the soft strands of a classical guitar filled the vehicle. If she had slept better last night, maybe she wouldn't feel so tired, though the doctor had told her fatigue wasn't unusual in the first trimester.

Less than a half hour later as they entered Lucas's town house, he said, "Go on upstairs. I'll bring you something to eat."

"You don't have to take care of me."

"I'm taking care of the baby," he responded. "Go on."

As Olivia climbed the steps, she was unable to tell if Lucas was still angry with her about last night, unable to tell what he was feeling at all.

When Lucas came up the stairs, he saw Olivia's bedroom door standing open. Last night he'd been frustrated when she'd pulled away, frustrated she couldn't see as clearly as he could where they were headed. And when she'd mentioned Whitcomb as if he was some paragon, Lucas had walked away to keep his temper in check. When she'd come to his room to tell him about Mim's call, he'd still wanted her in a physical way. He'd been gruff, because as her eyes had roved over his chest, he'd known he couldn't hide his need.

But when he'd gotten Molly Doyle's call today, fear had taken the place of frustration, anger *and* desire. What if something happened to Olivia and his baby? That fear had made him rush to her side and convince her to do what was best for her and their child whether she liked it or not.

The tea mug rattled against the glass of soda as he juggled them along with a plate holding half of a chicken sandwich. Olivia was standing at the dresser brushing her hair—long, shiny hair that was luxuriously thick and silky. She'd changed into knit slacks and a top that clung to just enough curves to make his desire rise again. He'd never had a problem keeping his libido in check before he'd seen Olivia at Barrington.

She turned as he came in and set her lunch on the

bedside stand. "Thank you," she said, her gaze meeting his. "I called Stanley to tell him I'd be out this afternoon."

After a brief silence, he asked, "Molly knows you're pregnant?"

Olivia sat on the edge of the bed. "I confided in her the day after I told you. I can trust her. She knows I'm staying here, too."

"Did you ask her to call me?"

With her pale cheeks becoming slightly rosy, she shook her head. "No. Molly does what she thinks is best no matter what anyone else says."

"Smart lady." He motioned to the sandwich. "Eat. And don't try to go to work again without eating breakfast. Got it?"

Her chin came up. "I can take care of myself."

The fact that she hadn't asked Molly to call him made him curt. "Well, you didn't do a very good job of it today, did you?"

Her defiance faded. "I won't let today happen again. I'll force a piece of toast down in the morning before I leave, and I'll get something for lunch even if it's only a cup of soup and crackers." She picked up the sandwich and took one nibble, and then another. "You don't have to watch to make certain I eat. I'm sure you want to get back to work."

"I'll work here this afternoon. I have a folder of printouts to analyze so Rex can decide what hotels he wants to acquire next."

When she'd finished the sandwich and sipped at the soda, she set her glass beside the tea mug. "I'm going to put my feet up for a while and rest. Don't feel that you have to stay."

He understood that she was used to being self-sufficient, but he wanted her to realize she didn't have to go through this pregnancy alone. "I'll be downstairs if you need anything."

Her lips still glistened with the moisture of the soda she'd drunk. He couldn't help running his thumb along her upper lip. Her eyes widened and he longed to kiss her and lie on the bed beside her. But she wasn't ready for that.

As he dropped his hand and turned to go, she said, "I appreciate everything you're doing for me and our baby."

"There's nothing I want more in this world, Olivia, than to be a father—and a good one. I know that starts now. Rest. I'll come up and check on you in a little while."

When Lucas closed Olivia's door, he realized he liked the idea of taking care of her. But as soon as the thought found a home in his heart, he warned himself to be careful. He remembered Celeste and her lies. Just because he liked the idea of being a daddy didn't mean he could let his guard down. Olivia could still be in love with her boss. She could still decide she wanted to raise this baby on her own.

He had to convince her that two parents were better than one and that forgetting about Stanley Whitcomb was in her best interest *and* their baby's.

Night had fallen when Lucas opened the door to Olivia's room, and light spilled inside. As she pushed herself up against the headboard, he crossed to her and handed her the cordless phone from his bedroom. "It's for you—your mother."

He'd been surprised when he'd answered it. He

didn't think Olivia had told anyone but Molly she was staying with him.

She switched on the bedside lamp and as she took the phone from him, she held her hand over the mouthpiece. "I had my calls forwarded."

That would explain it. But it was starting to bother him that she didn't want anyone to know she was staying here. Still, to give her privacy, he left the room and went downstairs. While she'd slept, he'd ordered groceries and had them delivered. The aroma of sauce simmering on the stove filled the house. He thought he might tempt Olivia's taste buds. If not, she could eat plain pasta.

He'd made a salad and put a crusty loaf of bread into the oven when she came into the kitchen. "Something smells good."

"It doesn't make you want to run in the other direction?"

"No. I'm actually hungry." She lifted the lid off the sauce, took a whiff and smiled. "You might have to give me your recipe. Did you go to the store?"

"Had it delivered."

"I can't believe I slept that long."

She still looked a bit sleepy, her hair softly ruffled. "Did you tell your mother you're staying with me?"

"Not yet. She wants to come up from Tucson this weekend for a visit. But I didn't want to make plans without checking with you."

"She'll be with you all weekend?"

"She'd like to drive over after school on Friday. She's a teacher."

"That will work great. There's someplace I should go this weekend." When he'd called Mim, she'd told him Trevor was having a tough time and not getting along with the other boys. She'd wondered if Lucas was coming for the weekend to give the nine-year-old some extra attention.

"Out of town?" Olivia asked.

He wasn't ready to tell her about the ranch and his background. Celeste hadn't understood how it drew him back or the responsibility of mentoring the boys there. "I'm going to visit friends in Flagstaff."

"When will you leave?"

"I'll fly up Friday after work."

"Then I'll call Mom back. While she visits this weekend, I'll tell her I'm pregnant."

"How will she take the news?"

"I don't know. I've always been responsible. I've tried never to give her a cause to worry."

"You're still responsible, Olivia. We both are. Make sure you tell her you're not in this alone."

"I will. I'll be back in a few minutes."

As Olivia left the kitchen, he realized he was getting used to her presence in his life. But he'd better not get too used to it until she decided whether or not they could be a family.

A few of Barrington's employees sat in the cafeteria Friday morning, drinking coffee and eating pastries before work. Cindy had called Olivia last night, asking her to meet her here. Olivia's red coatdress brushed her calves as she stepped inside. She'd felt like wearing something other than a suit today, telling herself she'd worn the red dress in celebration of Valentine's Day. But she was also hoping to see Lucas before he left. She'd been applying her makeup this morning when he'd called up the steps to say goodbye.

She felt rested today—better than she'd felt in weeks. When she'd returned to the town house last evening, she'd cooked supper. Lucas had come home around six, and they'd eaten and discussed their day. As she worked a needlepoint picture she hadn't touched in months, he'd read the newspaper and watched TV. When she'd said good-night, she'd thought he might kiss her again. But he hadn't. She'd wanted to question him about his "friends" in Flagstaff but didn't feel she had the right to pry.

When Olivia crossed the cafeteria with its salmon tiled floor, Formica-topped tables and sky-blue chairs, she spotted Rachel, Sophia, Molly, Patricia and Cindy in a far corner. Their expressions told her they were all waiting for her.

"Cindy has something to ask us," Molly explained. "But she wouldn't until you came."

Cindy smiled. Since her makeover that the five of them had given her for her thirtieth birthday, she wore bright colors and short skirts. Today she wore canary yellow. As soon as Olivia seated herself at the table between Sophia and Molly, Cindy leaned forward and spent a moment making direct eye contact with each of them.

"I want all of you to know how much I appreciate your friendship," she began. "Without it and without the makeover that you encouraged me to have, Kyle and I might not be engaged. Last night we checked with my church and some reception facilities, and we decided to get married on the third Saturday in November. I wanted to get together this morning to ask all of you to be in our wedding. Will you?"

A chorus of acceptances came from around the table.

"Thank you so much," Cindy said, her happiness evident in her wide green eyes. "Maybe we can go looking for gowns soon."

If they didn't shop soon, Olivia guessed she'd be starting to gain weight. Hopefully she could get back her figure after the baby was born in time for Cindy and Kyle's ceremony.

As they were discussing a possible color scheme for the wedding, Mike—Barrington's mailman—came over to their table with envelopes in his hand. His gaze fell on Sophia, but he addressed them all. "Ladies, I have invitations for you from Mr. Barrington."

In his chinos, polo shirt and short riding boots, Mike didn't quite fit in with the suited men employed at Barrington. His rakish good looks and "hunk" physique made him a common topic among single women in the office complex. But he was known as being a womanizer, out to have a good time.

He handed each of the women an envelope with a wink and a smile, but his fingers seemed to brush Sophia's with lingering intent as he handed her hers. Sophia's cheeks reddened.

Olivia opened her envelope and read the invitation. There would be a Valentine's Day party at three today in the cafeteria. The room would be closed from one to three for party preparations.

"How nice!" she commented, liking the way the Barrington Corporation treated everyone.

"Now I know why Mildred wanted a complete list of employees," Patricia said.

"*Everyone* has to come," Mike warned them. He leaned into their table and dropped his voice to a whisper. "I heard Rex even hired a DJ."

"Dancing?" Sophia asked.

"You bet. So, ladies," he drawled, "be ready to kick off those high heels. I'll see you all later," he added as he moved away.

As Sophia's gaze followed Mike, Olivia nudged her friend's elbow. "Are you interested?"

"He's sexy as sin with no spark of ambition." Sophia shook her head. "He might be the dreamiest man on the face of the earth, but I *can't* be interested. I need more than someone who's content to be a mailman."

Olivia knew Sophia's background, how she grew up in a poor section of town where she still lived with her mother. Financial security was important to her. "I think you've caught his eye."

"And he's caught mine. But that's as far as it goes. He'll have to take someone else for a ride on the back of his Harley."

Patricia stood. "I have to get to my office. 'The Third' is supposed to call this morning to discuss qualifications for his new assistant."

"I heard he has the sexiest voice," Rachel mused.

"But *no one's* ever seen him," Molly added. "I wonder how everything will change when he takes over Barrington."

Olivia rose to her feet, too, not as curious about Rex the Third as about Lucas's weekends in Flagstaff. "Cindy, just let me know when you want to go shopping. And thanks for asking me to be part of your wedding."

After Cindy hugged each of them, they all walked to the elevators. But instead of becoming involved in the conversations, Olivia wondered if Lucas would come to the party or if he'd leave early to begin his weekend.

Chapter Four

The Valentine's Day party was in full swing when Lucas entered the cafeteria at four o'clock. He'd wanted to clear his desk so he could leave directly from the party. As he scanned the room with its red paper cloths draping the tables, the silver and red hearts dangling from the fluorescent lights and the table with chafing dishes and a punch bowl, he realized he was looking for Olivia. He needed a glimpse of her before he left.

Music blared from speakers set up in a corner of the cafeteria where the DJ stood, and tables had been rearranged to make space for dancing. Employees were taking advantage of the DJ's selection—a rock 'n' roll favorite from the sixties. Suddenly he spotted Olivia at a table with Molly and...Whitcomb. Before he even thought once about it, let alone twice, he was crossing the room, knowing just a glimpse of Olivia wasn't enough.

Midway across the room, he slowed his stride. He

had to play this casually and act as if he was enjoying himself at the party like everyone else. Olivia wanted to avoid gossip and he respected that need, but it was going to be damn hard to act as if they were simply casual acquaintances.

Her gaze met his long before he reached the table. When he did, he gave them all a relaxed smile.

"Hello, Lucas," Molly said with a look that told him she knew exactly what was going on.

"Molly, Stanley, Olivia. It looks as if everyone who works at Barrington decided to party."

Stanley chuckled. "That invitation was a royal decree and everyone knows it. Rex has always believed employees socializing together now and then creates a more conducive atmosphere for work. I guess the last time he ordered Mildred to bring out the chafing dishes was the Christmas party."

Lucas's gaze collided with Olivia's. Then he cleared his throat and addressed Whitcomb. "I don't remember seeing you there."

"I could only stop in for a few minutes. My daughter was coming home from college and I had to pick her up at the airport."

Since Christmas Eve, he'd wondered why Olivia had fallen into conversation with him so easily that night, why she'd looked a bit lost—

What did she see in a man who had a daughter practically her own age?

A slow ballad replaced the drums and loud beat that had been emanating from the speakers.

"Now that's one worth dancing to," Whitcomb remarked as several couples made their way to the dance space.

Sensing what was about to happen, before Olivia's

boss took his observation any further, Lucas gazed directly into her eyes. "Would you like to dance?"

Her cheeks grew rosy and she smiled. "Sure."

Lucas pulled her chair out for her, wanting to take her in his arms then and there. But instead he let her precede him to the group of dancers. When they found an empty spot, he clasped her hand and drew her into his arms.

When she tensed, he suggested, "No one's going to notice two colleagues dancing for a few minutes. Just relax, Olivia, and enjoy the music and the moment."

They danced in silence for a short while, their breaths in unison, Olivia's perfume and the pretty curve of her lips tempting him to hold her close someplace other than a dance floor. He curbed the impulse as he should have on Christmas Eve after he'd kissed her under the mistletoe. But even with the impulse curbed, her breasts practically against his chest, her hand on his shoulder, her uncertain smile sending his hormones into a riot, made him take a deep breath.

"I guess you'll be spending the weekend at your apartment," he murmured.

"Until Mom leaves."

"Did you say she's a teacher?"

Olivia nodded. "Elementary school. She loves children. She'll be good with a grandchild. After she gets over the shock of the idea."

"Have you gotten over the shock?"

"I'm not sure. I've always imagined myself as a mother someday. But not this soon."

What would Olivia think of the ranch and the boys there? After his experience with Celeste, he was reluctant to tell Olivia about it and how he fit into the picture. But he would. Soon. And this weekend he'd tell Mim and Wyatt about the unexpected turn in his life.

As he danced with Olivia, he forgot they were merely supposed to be colleagues. Her body fit to his too well. Her red dress was slim, with buttons down the front, a silky fabric that slid against his thighs as they moved. When her hand on his shoulder rocked back and forth slightly to the rhythm of the music, her fingertips tauntingly near his neck held a sensual power over him. He remembered them stroking his back....

He pulled her closer and she didn't protest. When he bent his head, his lips were a whisper from her cheek. He could sense the softness of her skin before his jaw brushed it, tempting them both.

"Lucas..." Her voice trembled.

"What?" he murmured into her ear.

"Someone could be watching."

"There are too many people dancing for anyone to notice us." But as his cheek lingered against hers and he tested his self-control, he knew it was a dangerous game. If his lips came any closer to hers, everyone in the room would know they were more than co-workers.

Leaning back, he studied her. At least today she wasn't pale. "Any more dizziness?"

"No."

"Did you sleep last night?"

"Very well. Except...before I fell asleep, I was wondering how safe small planes are."

"As safe as the pilot and the condition of the plane. Worried I'll fall out of the sky?"

"That's not a joking matter."

More than most people, he knew the whimsy of split-second fate. He'd become an orphan in the blink of an eye. "I do everything I can to ensure my safety, whether I'm on the ground or in the air. But I don't think about it beyond that because I want to live my life without fear. Fear ties a man down. I need freedom and confidence when I take the plane up, not worry."

When she frowned, he realized she truly was concerned about him. "Flying is safer than driving. I'll take you up sometime."

All of a sudden, Olivia stiffened in his arms again and he saw why. Stanley was standing at the punch bowl, his gaze on them. Lucas felt his jaw clench.

The song ended and Lucas knew he should leave—he'd planned to leave—but the cogent temptation to stay was impossible to ignore.

Until Whitcomb stood at his side and tapped him on the shoulder. "Mind if I cut in?"

You're damn right, I mind, Lucas wanted to say. But Olivia didn't want gossip, and she might even prefer dancing with Stanley Whitcomb to dancing with him. Striving for a congeniality he wasn't feeling, he answered, "I have to be leaving anyway. Enjoy the party."

He heard Olivia's soft goodbye as he released her into the arms of another man. When he strode away without glancing at the couple again, he knew he should keep going, straight to Flagstaff.

Yet the devil on his shoulder stopped him at the doorway. He turned, and his stomach clenched. Stanley and Olivia were involved in a conversation as they danced—much too close for Lucas's peace of mind. They looked involved in each other, oblivious to

dancers surrounding them. With a succinct epithet
that would have traveled into the room but for the
music, he left the cafeteria, needing the wide spaces
of the ranch to think.

As Lucas didn't respond to her goodbye, Olivia let
Stanley lead her in a traditional box-step, trying not
to feel hurt. She never knew what to expect from
Lucas. When he'd asked her to dance, a thrill had
skipped up her spine. Being held by Lucas had ex-
hilarated her…excited her…until she realized Stanley
was watching them. And now in her boss's arms—
she felt no thrill. No excitement. Not even the comfort
of dancing with a man that she…admired? Respected? Just what *did* she feel for Stanley?

"Are you and Lucas an item?"

"I don't know what you mean."

"Be careful, Olivia. Lucas Hunter is a wild card."

"A what?"

"He sells himself to the highest bidder. Oh, he has
the skills to do it. Corporations clamor to hire him for
their next merger. But Hunter doesn't want to be tied
down anyplace for too long. In fact, I heard a New
York firm has been trying to hire him for the past two
years. They keep upping the offer."

This week as she'd lived with Lucas, she'd forgotten his reputation…his life-style. Just a few minutes
ago, he'd told her to relax and enjoy the moment.
That was so difficult for her. She always worried
about the future, wanting to plan it as best she could.
What if she considered marrying Lucas and he wanted
to take off from place to place like her father? What
if they married for the sake of the baby and then he
left after their child was born?

"Lucas seems to like working at Barrington," she said, hoping it was true.

"Lucas likes the work and he's not bored with it yet. But that doesn't mean he won't be in a few months. Just watch your step with him. I've heard rumors that he's involved with someone in Flagstaff."

Although her heart sank, she wanted to believe Lucas was really visiting friends. "Do you believe all the rumors that fly around here?"

"Of course not. But there *is* usually a grain of truth. I don't want to see you get hurt. He seemed proprietary when he took you to lunch the other day. That's why I'm cautioning you."

Lucas could be determined and forceful, but... "I can take care of myself, Stanley. You should know that by now."

"What I know is that you're a sweet young woman who has been working full-time and studying for the bar and doing an admirable job of both. But maybe now all of it is catching up to you and you need to take better care of yourself. You haven't missed a minute of work since you started here—until this week. That should tell you something."

It told her a lot. For the past months, she'd taken Stanley's advice and seen him as a mentor. Now she realized his caring attitude had been part of his nature, and she'd read more into it than was there. He was warning her away from Lucas because he honestly cared, not because he was jealous. And her feelings for him seemed to pale when she thought about the thrill that made her tremble when Lucas looked at her, or touched her.

"I appreciate your advice, Stanley. You know how much I respect your opinion."

"But you aren't going to listen to me, are you?" he asked, his forehead creasing with concern. "Either about slowing down *or* Lucas Hunter."

"You don't have to worry about me on either account."

Stanley shook his head and sighed. "Just like my daughter. She wants to make all her own decisions."

"Isn't that a good thing?" Olivia asked with a smile.

He chuckled. "Only if I agree with her decisions." After a pause, he asked, "Do you still want to stay late on Monday night?"

She'd forgotten she'd made plans with him for one last intense study session before the bar exam. In the past few weeks, he'd helped her remember anything she'd forgotten since August. With only a week and a half until the exam, she was grateful for his help. She suddenly wondered what Lucas would think, but decided it didn't matter. She had to do everything she could to prepare herself for this test.

"Monday night is still good. I'm getting more nervous as the exam gets closer."

With a smile he said, "We'll make sure you're ready."

As she gazed into Stanley's eyes and saw honest caring, she realized he was a good friend. And maybe that's what he'd always been—nothing more.

She thought about Lucas. Suddenly she was glad she was spending the weekend with her mother. Maybe she'd be able to help her sort everything out.

Dismounting from the pinto he usually rode, helping nine-year-old Trevor slide from the saddle to the ground, Lucas appreciated the cold air that filled his lungs, the snow-topped San Francisco peaks in the distance and the pine forests with their riding and hiking trails. The landscape here was so different from Phoenix, with its natural winter white and deep greens, aspen and bare cottonwoods. This had been the only home he'd ever known, yet not really home because he'd felt like a transient among five or six other boys who'd come and gone. He was the only one who'd stayed because no one had wanted to adopt him, and he'd had nowhere else to go. Only Mim and Wyatt's kindness had kept a roof over his head and food in his stomach.

He'd finally moved on and could give back some of the care they'd given him by spending time with the four boys who lived here now. Trevor had only been at the ranch a month and was having trouble settling in…fitting in. Lucas related all too well. He'd taken the boy for a morning ride, hoping he'd learn to feel at ease here.

"We have to groom the horses," Lucas said as Trevor started for the house about fifty yards from the barn and paddock.

"Can't you do it? I'm cold."

"It'll be warmer in the barn," Lucas remarked as he handed the reins of the gray to his small rider. Responsibility was the most important lesson to be learned at the ranch.

Trevor made a face, but took the reins and led Bullet into the barn.

"I'll help you, then you can help me," Lucas said as he put the horses into their stalls. Both horses were gentle but Lucas wanted to make sure Trevor didn't make any sudden moves that could cause an accident.

Night Song, a sorrel mare who was a favorite at the ranch, whinnied softly. Lucas rubbed her neck and ears. She was due to foal in a few weeks.

"You rode real well out there today." Lucas snagged the grooming brushes from a shelf on the wall and handed one to Trevor.

"I still can't go fast," Trevor mumbled.

He'd kept the horses at a walk so the boy wouldn't bounce off. With a shrug, Lucas suggested, "Give it time."

"I won't be here long. I'm goin' home to my mom." His almost-black eyes were defiant.

Home for Trevor had been a dirty room in a boardinghouse where he and his mother had gone hungry more often than not. It turned out that his mother didn't know how to read, and consequently couldn't hold down a job. Now she was staying at a group home and was enrolled in a literacy program that would hopefully lead to gainful employment. When Mim and Wyatt had heard about Trevor, they'd offered to take him in until his mother got her life together. Every Friday after school, Trevor could visit with her, then Wyatt brought him back to the ranch.

"Trevor, you're not here because you did something wrong. You know that, don't you?"

The boy looked away. "Then why'd they take me away from my mom?"

Lucas heard the catch in his voice despite his attempt to seem strong and disinterested most of the time. Capping the boy's shoulder, he nudged him around. "Your mom wants to make a better life for both of you. She needs more time to do that."

"I can help!"

"Yes, you can. By letting her know you're trying to be happy here while you're waiting."

"I don't *mean* like that," he snapped, the hood of his jacket falling back to his shoulders. His red cheeks, the thatch of black hair falling across his forehead and sad eyes made Lucas want to give him a great big hug. But Trevor was keeping his distance physically as well as emotionally.

Crouching down to Trevor's eye level, Lucas's hand tightened on the boy's shoulder. "I know it's hard only seeing your mom on Fridays. I know you want to stay in town with her, not come back out here. But she needs some time to concentrate on *her*. She needs to know you're okay and, just for now, you're managing without her."

"I *hate* living here. Kurt throws his stuff all over my bed. Jerry tries to tell me what to do, jus' because he's older than me. Russ is a baby. He always wants me to tie his shoes."

"He's only five and he looks up to you. He misses being with his mom, too." Right now, Russ's father, who had been abusive, was in a twelve-step program. But he still didn't have his drinking under control. On the other hand, Jerry's father had taken off for parts unknown and left his son with an uncle who had decided he couldn't take care of him. He had been at the ranch the longest, going on three years. And Kurt's mother was in a drug rehab program.

"What do *you* know about anything?" Trevor exploded, frustrated by Lucas's logic and feelings he didn't know how to handle.

Lucas didn't usually share his story, but this boy needed to see he had a lot more going for him than many others. "I came here when I was Russ's age because I didn't have a father, and my mother was killed in an accident. Mim and Wyatt took me in, just as they did you and Russ and Jerry and Kurt. I know what it feels like to lie awake at night wondering what's going to happen tomorrow. All I can tell you is that you're safe here, until your mom can take care of you again. And you might even find you like the other boys if you give them a chance."

Tears welled up in Trevor's eyes. "I want to go home."

"I know you do. And you will. But it's going to take some time."

The boy's chin quivered, and he wrenched away from Lucas's hand.

After Lucas straightened and gave him a few moments, he handed Trevor the grooming brush, knowing this boy like the others, needed something to do to feel he could make a difference, to feel needed here. Then maybe he could accept the fact that, for a few months at least, the ranch was his home.

Home.

Lucas wanted to make a home with Olivia. He hadn't yet told Mim and Wyatt he was going to be a father. Hopefully he could find a few quiet minutes with them tonight after the boys went to bed.

The strawberry ice cream in front of Olivia tempted her more than any food had all weekend. She and her mother had gone shopping and stopped at the ice cream parlor for old times' sake. When she was growing up, they didn't eat out often, but every Friday night they would go window shopping and stop for ice cream. Olivia dipped her spoon into her dish.

"You *are* going to tell me, aren't you?" her mother asked as she sipped her soft drink. Rosemary McGovern's auburn hair was permed into an attractive style around her face. In her early fifties, she was still a lovely woman. But right now she was a woman with a purpose.

"Tell you what?" Olivia had found the words *I'm pregnant* harder to say than she'd thought they'd be.

"Why you ate a piece of toast for breakfast instead of the oatmeal I fixed this morning. Why you ordered lemonade instead of cola. Why I found a new type of vitamins in your cupboard. If I didn't know better, I'd think…"

Before her mother put it into words, she responded, "I'm pregnant."

Her mother blinked twice, then finally asked, "The man who answered the phone the other night?"

"His name is Lucas Hunter. He works at Barrington, too."

After a pensive pause, she studied her daughter closely. "I see. And what about Stanley Whitcomb? I thought you had your cap set for him."

"Mother…"

"Don't you *Mother* me. You mentioned him often enough with determination in your voice. What happened?"

She had never lied to her mother and she wouldn't start now. "Lucas happened. On Christmas Eve. I'm still not sure why I…why I…let it happen."

"What's he like?" her mother asked gently.

A warmth welled up in Olivia's heart. "He's tall and handsome and so…" She might as well just admit it. "Sexy."

Her mother smiled. "Anything else?"

Olivia took a spoonful of ice cream. "He can be stubborn and very determined, evasive, gentle and sweet, too."

"And how does he feel about your being pregnant?"

"He wants me to marry him. He wants to be a father. But, Mom, he's not staid and stable and dependable like Stanley. Lucas might not even want to stay in Phoenix. He owns a plane, flies off on business or a whim, and I'm afraid he might be more like Dad than I care to admit."

"He wants to chase a dream?"

"I don't know what his dreams are," Olivia confessed.

"A man's dreams are very important, honey. Your dad had and still *has* dreams made of smoke. Even if he could reach one, he'd never hold on to it because he'd think he could find one better. If you discover this man's dreams, you'll really know the man."

Swishing her spoon absently in her ice cream, Olivia admitted, "I thought Stanley would be the perfect husband. That's why I was interested."

"Was?"

"I moved in with Lucas to get to know him. No strings. No ties. Not yet. And I've only been there a week. He's complicated."

"And so are you." She took Olivia's hand. "Honey, a boring man doesn't guarantee happiness any more than an ardent attraction can provide permanence. Only your heart knows the *right* answer for you. But you have to listen carefully and wait until you can hear it. Just because you're pregnant doesn't mean you have to rush into anything."

"I know. And I won't. Everything has happened so fast."

"Give your world a chance to stop spinning. And know that I'm here if you need me."

Olivia understood how fortunate she was to always have her mother in her corner. Her dad might have chased his dreams all these years, but her mother had given her the opportunity to make realistic dreams come true. She simply had to figure out if and how Lucas fit into them.

Lucas entered his town house, his senses on the alert for Olivia. He hadn't spotted her car where she usually parked it. When he stepped into his living room, her absence was tangible. He'd returned earlier than usual, anxious to touch down in Scottsdale. That eagerness was unusual.

He tried to read the Sunday paper, but his attention wandered to his conversation with Mim and Wyatt. They wanted to meet Olivia but understood his reluctance to spring the ranch on her after his experience with Celeste. What if Olivia wanted no part of it? The boys were important to his life, too. He figured a few more weeks, after he and Olivia had connected a little better…

When the door opened, he took a deep breath and casually folded the paper on the hassock.

"Oh! You're back," Olivia said as she saw him.

Since he'd parked in the private garage behind the building, she couldn't have known. Yet he'd hoped for something a little more enthusiastic. Had her conversation with Whitcomb developed into more than a dance?

She looked like a teenager in her jeans and T-shirt,

with her hair tied back in a ponytail. "Did your mother leave?" he asked.

Olivia dropped a bag onto the sofa. "We went shopping, then she left from the mall. She insisted on buying me something for the baby."

"How did she react when you told her?"

"My mother's special, Lucas. She was surprised, but...supportive. As she always is. She just wants me to be careful in the decisions I make right now."

"About me?"

"About everything. How was your weekend?"

"Fine."

"Just fine?"

"It's always good to get away. Flagstaff is very different from Phoenix. There's snow on the ground."

"Did you go skiing?"

Arizona Snow Bowl, less than a half hour from the ranch, offered runs. But the ranch had always held more allure than the slopes. "Not this time."

Reaching to the sofa, he snagged the bag. "Can I look?"

"Sure."

The yellow shirt and pants and the tiny booties looked as if they'd fit a doll, not a child. "They're so small!"

She laughed. "They're three months. Mom said you should always buy clothes too big."

"Big? My gosh..." He suddenly realized this child was fragile and needed so much more protection than he'd ever imagined.

"It's scary, isn't it?" Laying her hand on her stomach, Olivia got a dreamy look in her eyes. "I haven't felt any movement and probably won't for a couple of months. Yet I'm always aware there's a new life inside me. Like I can sense that tiny heartbeat. And when Mom bought these… Lucas, our child will fit into these clothes, go to kindergarten, hopefully college someday. I just can't wait for each moment of it!''

His heart contracted with emotions he couldn't name as he stood. ''You really want this baby, don't you?'' He'd been so afraid Olivia would blame him for the pregnancy and think of their child as a burden rather than a joy, a responsibility that would complicate her career and her relationship with Whitcomb.

''Want it? More than anything,'' she said fervently.

Facing her, he looked directly into her eyes. ''It's been a week. What about us?''

She hesitated for a few seconds. ''I think we still have a long way to go.''

His chest tightened, and he remembered she could walk out of his life at any time and take their child with her. Maybe straight to Stanley Whitcomb.

Chapter Five

Olivia had been truthful, but Lucas's expression said he didn't like her conclusion.

"A long way to go until what?" he asked. "Until you forget about the life you had planned before you learned you were pregnant? I'm beginning to wonder if you *can* forget."

"I still want a career," she returned after a tense moment. "I still want to pass the bar and practice law. If you think that no longer matters—"

The phone rang, cutting her off. But she ignored it, needing to say what was on her mind. "I still don't know much about *you*. Your background. Your dreams. We—"

The ringing continued.

"I'd better get that," Lucas said, reaching for the phone.

She thought he looked relieved at the interruption. What wasn't he telling her? Why did he keep so guarded? Where had he really gone over the weekend and who had he spent it with? All were answers she needed before they could move forward.

As Lucas answered the phone and listened to the speaker, his stance became vigilant. He was absorbing information and processing it. Finally he said, ''We'll get this ironed out. We've put too much time and energy into the offer to have negotiations fall apart now. Don't worry. I'll be there as soon as I can.''

''Trouble?'' she asked when he'd hung up.

''It was Rex. The deal's going sour and we have to plan a new strategy.'' He headed for the stairs. ''I have to change. I'll probably be in meetings all night.''

As he took the first three steps, she called to him. ''Lucas?''

He stopped.

''We have to talk.''

His hand on the banister, his look of purpose changed to one she couldn't read. ''Tomorrow night. We'll go somewhere quiet for supper—''

''I can't tomorrow night. Stanley's going to help me study for the bar exam. I only have this week to make sure I've got everything down pat.''

Lucas's jaw set. ''I see. Well, you let me know when you can fit me into your schedule. Right now mine is tight.'' He climbed the remainder of the steps and closed the door to his room.

Olivia's mother had taught her not to swear. Ladies shouldn't swear. But Olivia remembered a string of words she'd heard her father use. She used them now under her breath with as much vehemence as a whisper would allow. Then she concluded that Lucas Hunter was the most frustrating man on the face of the earth.

And she was falling in love with him.

As the sun rose Monday morning, Olivia felt something was amiss. It took her a few moments to realize she'd been awake on and off throughout the night listening for Lucas—his footfalls, the creak of his mattress, the sound of water running in the bathroom. But she'd heard none of those noises. Sliding out of bed and snatching up her robe, she went to his bedroom. The door was closed.

When she knocked, there was no answer. Opening it, she found a bed without a wrinkle. He hadn't slept in it last night. She told herself maybe he'd returned late and left early, but she knew better. There was no trace of his cologne, no sense of his presence.

Quickly dressing, she ate a piece of toast and hurried to her car. During the drive to Barrington, she realized she could have tried to call him. But she didn't want him to think she was checking up on him. At the complex, she could stop at his office and make discreet inquiries if he wasn't there. If he wasn't at Barrington...

Maybe he'd flown off to visit his "friend" again—a friend who didn't have study sessions with her boss.

At Barrington, Olivia found a spot close to the front entrance and took it. The deep salmon concrete building rose against the turquoise sky as a few puffy clouds hung suspended like huge cotton balls. As she passed saguaro cactus and teddy bear cholla, she appreciated the warmth of the sun on her hair. Phoenix in February had to be one of the best spots on earth. She paused only a moment in the three-story-high foyer, then headed for the elevators giving access to the east wing. She'd check his office first.

She was early enough that not many employees milled about. Her heart thumped faster as she exited the elevator and made a beeline for Lucas's office. Then she forced herself to slow down. Wet-floor placards lined the tiled hall. Making certain each step in her high heels was a sure one, she reached Lucas's door and took a deep breath. When she knocked, she waited for a response. Not getting one, she turned the knob and found the door unlocked.

At first, she thought his office was empty. But then her gaze fell on stockinged feet, and the rest of Lucas stretched out on the couch. His cuffs were unbuttoned, his white shirt wrinkled, his tie tugged down and askew. As she quietly rounded the desk to get a better look, he opened his eyes. They were hazy with sleep.

"Good morning," she said softly, not sure what response she was going to get.

He swung his feet to the floor and sat up, looking sexily rumpled. His beard shadow added to the effect as he checked his watch, then stretched his neck as if he had a crick in it. "You're here early."

"I was worried. I didn't know whether you got tied up or if you just decided not to come home."

"We met late into the night, then I had to work out language for the contracts. Maybe I should have called, but I didn't want to wake you if you were asleep."

"I didn't sleep very well because I knew you weren't there," she admitted.

He studied her for a short while, then rolled his head again and winced.

"I can help work that out," she suggested.

"It'll be fine," he said gruffly.

"Let me try." She needed to feel close to him again, to dissolve not only the tension in his shoulders, but between them. Coming up beside him, she placed a hand on his shoulder. "Turn sideways."

This time he didn't argue.

"If you take your shirt off, I can find the knots better."

"You won't have far to look," he muttered as he tugged off his tie. Then he swiftly pulled out his shirt from his waistband, unfastened the buttons and shrugged it off.

The broad expanse of his shoulders and back, all that roped strength, taut muscle and tan skin beckoned to her and started a slow burn in her belly. When her fingertips inched onto his shoulders, the heat of his skin spread to her hands, arms, all of her. But it wasn't a heat she wanted to escape. Her thumbs kneaded the knots, but her other fingers gloried in the texture of his skin while she breathed in his scent.

As she worked his shoulders, he groaned and dropped his head, giving her all the access she wanted. His neck tempted her, not to continue the massage but to place soft kisses there. What was wrong with her? Why did she feel like melting at his feet? Because he hadn't gone somewhere else last night? Was she simply feeling relief?

Uh-uh. Relief definitely wasn't the feeling curling through her like liquid fire.

When she slid her fingers into his hair at his nape, he straightened and turned, catching her hand.

"That's enough." His voice was husky, his eyes a piercing blue.

"I wasn't finished," she murmured, unable to move or breathe or figure out what about him compelled her to be impulsive, to want with a passion that was dangerous to her plans and common sense.

"If I let you *finish,* neither of us will get to work anytime soon."

The desire in his eyes brought back visions of Christmas Eve, clothes discarded in haste and fiery kisses that created frightening yet exciting needs. Trying to calm her imagination and her memories, she asked, "Are you going home?"

He rose to his feet and checked his watch again. "No. I have clean shirts and a razor in the closet. In fifteen minutes I have to be in the executive suite for another meeting."

The hair on his chest as well as the whorl above his belt buckle drew her gaze.

"Will you be home for supper, or is that included in your study session?" he asked evenly.

"Stanley knows a deli that delivers."

"I'll bet he does," Lucas grumbled as he went to the closet and grabbed a shirt from a hanger. The hanger fell to the floor and he left it there. "So what time will you be home?"

"Around nine."

"I'll see you then." Breaking eye contact, he buttoned his shirt, dismissing her.

The tension between them was thicker than ever. Before he switched on his razor and shut her out completely, she turned and left. She'd worked long and hard to become a lawyer; she wouldn't let one frustrating but sexy male stop her now.

Although Lucas sat in front of his laptop in the kitchen, he checked the clock every fifteen minutes. It was well after nine when he switched it off and began pacing. Olivia came in the door at nine-thirty, and he didn't know whether to pick up the remote and pretend as if he was going to watch TV or ask her questions that she probably wouldn't answer.

He opted for a grumble. "Long study session."

Setting the study guide and notebooks on the end table, she looked up. "It was the last one. I have the rest of this week and the weekend to make sure I remember everything that I knew last summer."

"You'll do fine."

"I don't know that, Lucas. No one does. Not until notification comes." After a cautious glance at him, she added, "Stanley thinks I should stay at a hotel within walking distance for the test, and I think he's right."

"It's not that far."

"I can't take any chances. I've studied for years for this opportunity and had to wait six months because a quirk of fate made me miss it in August. Stanley says he's even heard of people getting held up in elevators. I'm not going to let anything keep me from the test this time."

"He's making you paranoid," Lucas snapped, not liking the idea of her staying in a hotel room, not liking her acting as if Stanley's advice was the law.

"He's *not* making me paranoid. You should understand what taking the bar and passing it means. And without Stanley—"

His expression must have stopped her, though he thought he was guarding volatile feelings really well. Until this moment. "Go on, Olivia. What about without Stanley? Do you think you'll be able to do without him?"

Olivia straightened, squared her shoulders and glared at him. "Exactly what does *that* mean?"

Against his better judgment, he stepped close to her. "*If* we're considering marriage, and I was under the impression that was why we were living together, you can't wear your heart on your sleeve around Stanley Whitcomb!"

"I *don't*."

"Oh, yes, you do. I see the looks you give him. I saw you dancing with him, how intimate the conversation was. You two were so intense, a firebomb couldn't have separated you. What's it going to take to make you forget about him?"

When she seemed to be at a loss for words, he decided he knew the answer. With a possessive demand that had plagued him all weekend, he crushed her to him and kissed her as if the world was going to end in the immediate future.

Kissing Olivia had been a trip to the stars from the first touch of lips on lips. But tonight the explosion shook him in an elemental way that almost frightened him. Why? Because he was fighting to create the family he'd never had? Because she was so sweet and lovely and full of passion? Because she was carrying his child? Because the stakes this time went beyond high risk, beyond satisfying a physical need, beyond the next morning?

He slid his hands under her suit jacket, stroking up her sides to her breasts. As his tongue thrust into her mouth, he heard her soft moan and felt her melt into his hands. He wanted her naked, under him, in his bed, with a wedding ring on her finger.

But as he let the vision and desires sweep away the

frustration of keeping his distance, she tore her mouth from his and pushed back.

Her color was high, her eyes sparkling, her lips rosy with that just-kissed look. "Stanley has been my mentor and my friend, and I'm not going to feel guilty about that. I'm not sure what you want from me, Lucas. You can't just take over my life. Why should you be jealous of my feelings for Stanley when you fly off on weekends to see some woman?"

Absorbed by the fact that she'd admitted having feelings for her boss, it took him a moment to grasp the rest of what she'd said. She thought he was involved with someone. "Where did you get *that* idea?"

"Everyone at Barrington knows—"

"*No one* at Barrington knows what I do on weekends. It has nothing to do with a woman."

"A woman called here asking for you." The questions in Olivia's eyes demanded answers.

Raking his hand through his hair, he realized he had to let Olivia into the life that he kept private for a multitude of reasons. Even so, he hesitated to get into his background, to spring the enormity of his commitment to the ranch on her.

"Lucas, I can't imagine more than being roommates if you won't let me get to know you."

It was an ultimatum of sorts, yet it carried an honesty he couldn't deny. "The woman who called was Mim Carson. She and her husband, Wyatt, were my foster parents. They have a ranch outside of Flagstaff, and that's where I go most weekends to help out with the boys who are staying there now."

Olivia's eyes grew wider and greener, then became lit by the smile that curved up her lips. "That's wonderful, Lucas. Why didn't you just tell me about it before? Why don't you want anyone to know?''

"I don't intentionally keep it a secret. No one ever asked me outright. It's just much simpler to say I'm visiting friends.''

She sank down on the sofa. "That doesn't explain why you didn't tell *me*.''

When he sat beside her, he thought about Celeste. "The ranch means a lot to me. Without Mim and Wyatt, I don't know where I would have ended up. I didn't have a father. My mother got pregnant when she was young, and he wanted nothing to do with us. She was killed in an automobile accident when I was five and I had no living relatives. Mim and Wyatt took me in.''

Olivia laid her hand on his arm. "I'm so sorry.''

He shrugged. "I had a good life.''

"That doesn't make up for your loss.''

Her empathy was important but he wasn't sure she understood. "I feel I need to give something back, to thank Mim and Wyatt for giving me a chance at a successful life. They didn't laugh when I told them I wanted to be a lawyer. Instead, they encouraged me and discovered a foundation where I applied for a grant. I graduated debt-free, Olivia. I've been so fortunate, and I want to teach the boys who are there now that they can reach their dreams, too.''

Her fingers squeezed his arm. "Why didn't you want to tell me?''

"Because I'm committed to them. I didn't know how you'd feel about that.''

After studying him for a few moments, she asked, "When are you going to the ranch again?''

"That depends. Would you like to come along?''

"Very much," she said softly.

If he played his cards right, he could prove to her she didn't need Whitcomb in her life...even as a mentor. "I'll stay home this weekend, and we'll make sure you're prepared for the bar exam. Next weekend we can both go to the ranch. What do you think?"

"Are you sure you want to help me? You could be in the mountains doing whatever you do—"

"Let me be your coach. It will be good practice for when you're in labor."

She laughed. "I'm not sure we should compare the two. But if you're sure..."

"I'm sure."

Keeping her gaze on his, she said, "Lucas, Stanley is...a friend. He helped me with studying tonight. That's all."

Lucas wished he could believe that but wondered if she was denying her feelings for her boss because of the pregnancy.

Only time would tell.

Just as next weekend would tell whether or not Olivia could accept his commitment to the ranch.

Deep coral and shades of pink streaked the sky as dusk enveloped the McDowell Mountains on Sunday evening. Out on Lucas's terrace, Olivia answered a question he had posed to her on constitutional law. As she finished, he snapped shut the study guide.

"That's it, lady. You're ready. No more studying."

The past week, they had settled into a routine. Most nights they'd gotten home from work at the same time and cooked supper together. They'd even eaten in the dining room—Lucas had admitted that was the first he'd used it—and they'd discussed mainly their work, but other aspects of their lives, too. She'd revealed that her parents were divorced. He'd given her background on the boys at the ranch in Flagstaff. Although he was more open to her questions now, she still felt his guardedness when he talked about the ranch. When he'd settled with work, TV or the newspaper, she'd studied in her room.

Since their explosive kiss on Monday, he hadn't touched her. Because when they kissed, she'd pushed away? Because he thought she loved Stanley? Because if they kissed again, they wouldn't stop with a kiss?

Now watching the breeze ruffle Lucas's hair, she said, "Thank you. You've been a terrific help."

Leaning forward, he asked, "Do you feel confident?"

"Mainly I feel scared. I can't tell if the butterflies in my stomach are because of the baby or the exam!"

He laughed. "Probably both."

When the telephone rang, Lucas said, "I'll get it."

But Olivia followed him inside. The temperature was dropping and her sweater wasn't enough protection.

Lucas answered the phone, then frowned and handed it to her. "It's Whitcomb."

Thankful for call-forwarding, she took the phone and noticed Lucas didn't move into the other room, but casually lounged at the counter watching her.

"Hi, Stanley,"

"Was that Lucas?" her boss asked.

"Yes, it was."

"I see. I was calling, thinking I'd bring over some fried chicken in case you'd buried yourself in preparation for the bar and forgotten to eat."

"That's so thoughtful of you. But I already ate."

"You *did* study?"

She knew what he was thinking since Lucas had answered. "Most of the weekend. I won't let you or Barrington down."

"I have every confidence in you, Olivia. Do you need time off tomorrow?"

"No. It's better if I stay busy. I'll work my usual hours then check in at the motel tomorrow evening."

"Olivia, remember what I told you about Lucas."

"I will. Thanks for thinking about me."

When she hung up, Lucas hadn't moved. "He wanted to take you to dinner?"

"He was going to bring something by if I hadn't taken time to eat."

"He knows you pretty well."

"I've been working with him a while. Part-time when I was in school, full-time since."

"You didn't tell him you're living with me or even that I helped you study."

It seemed like an accusation rather than a comment. "Why should I? It's my business, not his."

"What else is going on?"

"*Nothing* is going on." She couldn't tell him Stanley disapproved of her seeing him, that he had only voiced her own doubts aloud. No, Lucas wasn't seeing another woman. But she still didn't know if he wanted the same permanency she did.

As Lucas straightened, the nerve in his jaw worked. "You're hiding your head in the sand, Olivia. You have decisions to make. Don't delude yourself into thinking your life is the same as it was before Christmas Eve."

"Nobody knows better than I do what happened

Christmas Eve. But I don't *make* a decision until I'm sure I'm making the *right* decision. And I don't appreciate being grilled every time Stanley's name comes up.''

"Fine," Lucas snapped. "No more grilling. Just remember that's *my* baby you're carrying."

After Lucas strode away from her, she wanted to call him back. But she didn't. Maybe after she took the bar, the road would seem straighter, maybe she could relax, maybe she could understand her feelings for Lucas that had seemed to spring up in the blink of an eye.

Or in a moment of making love.

Frustrated desire was no reason to lose patience with Olivia, Lucas reminded himself for the umpteenth time as he carried the basket to the second floor of the modest motel where she was staying. Sometimes he wanted to shake or kiss the caution right out of her.

Definitely kiss.

After Stanley's call, they'd gone their separate ways. He still remembered the scent of her bubble bath lingering in the bathroom before he'd turned in. Tempted to knock on her door, he'd decided against it. This morning they'd awkwardly skittered around each other. He'd left first, and he was sure she'd breathed a sigh of relief. Not a good way to prove they were compatible...that she should forget about Whitcomb.

Lucas had never been the jealous type, but where Olivia was concerned...

The explanation was simple. She was the mother of his child.

Rapping on her motel room door, he didn't like the idea that a bribe had convinced the desk clerk to give him her room number. Though he'd wanted to reserve her a room at a four-star hotel and pay for it himself, he'd known Olivia would never accept it.

It took her a minute to open the door, and he guessed she had looked through the peephole first. He hoped she had.

"Lucas! What are you doing here?"

He couldn't tell if she was pleased to see him or not. But she was definitely pale, and he suspected the stress of waiting and anticipating was getting to her. That's why he'd come.

"I brought you something," he said with a smile, lifting the basket. "Can I come in?"

"Sure," she replied, opening the door wide and letting him inside.

He set the basket on the bed and motioned to it. "Open it."

Still looking perplexed, Olivia untied the pink ribbon holding the paper in a bunch at the top. As she brushed the wrap aside, she stared at the contents.

Lucas explained. "It's a bar exam survival kit. Crackers for the butterflies in your stomach, bubble bath to help you relax, writing paper in case there's someone you want to write to, those square things are supposed to make your drawers smell good and last but not least—a book I thought you'd enjoy."

When Olivia picked up the book with a child on the cover, entitled *Your Child's First Year,* her chin quivered and tears spilled down her cheeks.

Clasping her shoulders, he turned her toward him. "What's wrong? I thought this might help—"

"Oh, Lucas, it's so sweet. I can't believe you did this."

Sliding his hand under her hair, he tipped her chin up. "Then why the tears?"

"I don't know! I just..." Her breath caught in a sob.

He pulled her into his arms and held her tight. "Let it out, Olivia. It's okay. Everything's going to be okay."

While she cried, he held her close and stroked her hair. He'd bought two books last week on women and pregnancy, and he'd bet her mood had as much to do with the chemical changes in her body as with stress. As he'd read, he'd been amazed at the changes a woman's body goes through as she prepares to give birth. To his surprise he'd also read that a pregnant woman shouldn't fly in an airplane cabin that wasn't pressurized. Since his wasn't, oxygen deprivation could be a problem for her and the baby. They'd have to drive to Flagstaff over the weekend. He'd been disappointed he couldn't take her flying until after the baby was born. But her safety and his child's was more important than a thrill she could experience in the future.

After a few minutes, she pushed away, looking totally embarrassed. "I'm sorry. I don't know what's wrong with me. It must be hormones."

He tenderly wiped a few tears from her cheek with his thumb. "Taking the bar exam is stressful when nothing else is going on in your life, let alone when your plate is full. There's nothing to apologize for."

Going to the nightstand, she plucked a tissue from the box and blew her nose. Then her gaze shyly met his. "I probably look a sight."

Her nose was red and so were her cheeks. But her green eyes sparkled and she looked more relaxed. "You're beautiful as always. And just perfect for dinner in a quiet restaurant and a walk that will help you sleep."

"I am a little hungry. I was trying to decide what to do about dinner before you knocked."

"Now we can do it together."

Lucas waited while Olivia washed her face and brushed her hair. As he helped her with her sweater coat, he struggled against his desire to kiss her. They ate at the small restaurant attached to the motel, their gazes connecting often, their knees grazing each other now and then. Her jeans against his created a friction that made him take a drink of cold water more than once. He told her what he'd read about flying during pregnancy, explaining the difference between riding in a small plane that didn't have a pressurized cabin and a commercial jet that did. They agreed not to take any chances and to drive to Flagstaff.

After supper they walked, picking out constellations, glancing at each other under the streetlights, listening to the palm fronds shift in the breeze. When they returned to the motel, they climbed the steps to her room.

After she unlocked her door, she asked, "Do you want to come in?"

He wanted to take her in his arms and put one of those double beds in her room to good use. But this wasn't the night to recreate the passion they'd shared on Christmas Eve. "I'd better let you get to bed. You'll probably have your alarm set for dawn to make sure you're there in plenty of time."

"And a wake-up call soon after," she admitted

with a wide smile. Then she did something he absolutely did not expect. Linking her arms around his neck, she kissed him on the cheek with a gentle passion that made his heart race.

But before he could react, she settled back on her sneakers and smiled. "Thank you for tonight, Lucas. You are a *very* nice man."

To keep in the mood, he leaned close to her and whispered in her ear, "Don't tell anyone. You'll blow my cover." Kissing her full on the lips quickly, he backed away. "Good luck tomorrow."

With another smile and a nod, she went inside. Right before she crossed the threshold, he called, "Don't forget the chain lock."

Making a face at him, she closed the door.

A moment later he heard the rattle of the chain.

He smiled and then felt it slip away as he realized he didn't like the idea of going back to his town house knowing Olivia wouldn't be there.

What in the world was happening to him?

In less than nine months he'd be a father. That was enough to rattle anyone.

Chapter Six

From the passenger's seat in Lucas's Jeep, Olivia watched the desert colors slip by as they drove from Phoenix to Flagstaff. She'd brought soda and crackers for the two-hour drive and offered both to Lucas. With a smile, he'd taken the soda.

He'd met her at the motel again on Tuesday after the first day of testing. As they'd eaten and walked, they'd discussed the questions and her answers. He'd kissed her at the door and left her tingling with desire that had invaded her dreams. And on Wednesday when she'd returned home from the second day of exams, he'd bought her a bouquet of pink sweetheart roses and made dinner!

He was courting her and she loved it. But was he doing it because of the baby or because he had genuine feelings for *her*?

After taking a few swallows of soda, he set the can in the holder. "If you want to stop and stretch anytime, just say so."

"I'm fine. But I'll let you know if I need to move around."

They'd driven to Barrington together this morning and left together. But no one had seemed to notice. As the road curved before them, Olivia decided she should tell Lucas about the most exciting part of her day—up until the moment she'd left with him.

"Mr. Barrington called me this afternoon."

Lucas glanced at her. "Rex? What did he want?"

"He must keep close tabs on all his employees. He said that he'd heard I'd taken the bar exam and he wanted to remind me that after I receive notification that I've passed, there would be a position for me at Barrington. Stanley had handed in my evaluations and Mr. Barrington assured me they were both pleased with my work. Isn't that terrific?"

Instead of the matching excitement she expected from Lucas, he frowned. "And what did you tell him?"

"I told him I would be delighted to be an official member of the legal department at Barrington. If I pass."

The sound of the car on the road emphasized Lucas's silence until he asked, "And what about our baby?"

"What about our baby?" Olivia didn't understand the hard edge in Lucas's question.

"Our child deserves a full-time mother, not a woman who gives her best at work and leaves left-overs for her family."

She hadn't really thought about her work in regards to her child. For so long she had been focused on her education, passing the bar, finding a good position.

"You want me to waste all the years I studied and worked for this?"

"I want you to realize you're going to be a mother with a different set of priorities."

"And just why can't I be both?" She felt her temper rising and her defenses clanging firmly in place.

Lucas shook his head. "I don't see how that's possible. I don't see how you can give a child what he needs when you're not there."

"So all the responsibility falls on me?"

"No. Of course not. But especially for the first six months—do you want a stranger caring for our child?"

The shock of being a mother was still so new to her, she hadn't thought beyond looking forward to feeling her baby move the first time. When she thought about labor and delivery, she mostly felt frightened. She hadn't yet read the book Lucas had bought for her on the first year of a child's life, and she wondered if he had.

"When are you going to tell Rex you're pregnant?" he asked. "Or were you planning on working up until the day you deliver and return the day afterward?"

"Don't be ridiculous!"

"You have to make some decisions, Olivia. And you have to make them soon."

The briskness in Lucas's tone urged her to take a good look at him. She couldn't see his eyes behind his sunglasses. His arm was tense as he held the wheel. Was he the type of man who always had to get his own way? Who couldn't see her point of view? Did she really know him any better today than the day she'd moved in with him?

She knew more about him. But did she really know what drove him, what he wanted in life besides being a father? Maybe this weekend would give her some answers.

The landscape changed but Lucas's profile and his set jaw did not. Instead of palms swaying in bunches or rows, fir trees rose high, forestful after forestful. Snow had melted from the road, but the fields were still white. Lucas switched on a CD and Olivia tried to relax to the music. But besides the tension between her and Lucas, she was becoming more nervous about the weekend. What if these people didn't like her? What if they'd already made a moral judgment about her?

As they approached Flagstaff, she took another glance at Lucas. They'd changed into comfortable clothes before they'd left Barrington. Lucas's snap-button shirt, jeans and black boots, his suede jacket and black Stetson tossed into the back seat of the Jeep, reminded her he had many facets she didn't know.

Eventually Lucas turned off the main highway. After a mile or so he made a right onto a snow-packed road. In the headlights, she caught glimpses of fence lining the white fields and snow lying heavy on pine boughs. A house came into view, a bright porch light illuminating the front. Different from the adobe and red-tiled buildings in Phoenix, it looked as she imagined a ranch house would look. It was tall and square with a portion sticking out from the side that must be an addition. White with black shutters, its wrap-around front porch gave it a welcoming air.

She hoped she wasn't letting her imagination run away with her.

A huge floodlight glowed atop a large white barn and cast shadows on another building that looked like a garage.

Parking at the front walk, Lucas glanced down at her sneakers. When he climbed out, he opened the back door and shrugged into his jacket, setting the Stetson on his head. Quickly Olivia grabbed the colorful, Navaho-pattern wool jacket she'd bought yesterday, and slid it on before she got out. Lucas was beside her as they started up the snow-packed walk. As her foot slipped on ice, he caught her elbow and before she realized his intention, he scooped her up in his arms.

"Lucas, what will everybody think—"

"You care too much what everybody thinks. Would you rather fall?"

She knew he was thinking of the baby. "No. But you're not going to carry me around all weekend, either."

"I'm sure Mim has a pair of old boots. You're about the same size." With that, he carried her up the walk and didn't stop until he'd mounted the porch steps and deposited her at the door.

His Stetson shadowed his eyes and when he stepped away, she had no idea what he was thinking. She hated this discord between them, the silence that wouldn't be filled with surface conversation. She'd discovered when something was bothering Lucas, he didn't talk unless he had something decisive to say.

He didn't ring the bell or knock, but walked right in. No sooner had they stepped inside, than she heard pairs of scurrying feet. A young voice called, "Lucas, is that you?"

A few moments later they were surrounded by four

boys who were studying her carefully. As she smiled at them, a couple came into the living room.

"Everyone, this is Olivia," Lucas said. As he capped each boy's head and ruffled their hair, he began, "This is Jerry, Russ, Kurt and Trevor."

The woman came forward, gave Lucas a hug and extended her hand to Olivia. "I'm Mim Carson. This is my husband, Wyatt. We're glad you could come."

Mim's hair was as black as onyx with fine lines of gray running through it. It was longer than Olivia's but completely straight and banded in a low ponytail. Her high cheekbones spoke of Native American ancestry. When she squeezed Olivia's hand, hers was warm, her dark brown eyes welcoming.

"It's a pleasure to meet you," Olivia replied, meaning it.

Wyatt took her hand then and pumped vigorously. "Lucas didn't tell us you were a real beauty." His brown eyes twinkled under heavy brown brows. He was a burly man with a beard, as tall as Lucas.

Before she could respond, the smallest boy, Russ, tugged on Lucas's arm. "Can you take us riding tomorrow? Please?"

The boy who was standing on the edge of the welcoming circle—Trevor, she remembered—wrinkled his nose. "Don't be a twit. He'll probably take *her*."

There was silence as Lucas took off his hat and hung it on the rack by the door. Then he said to Trevor, "I promised I would take all of you riding the next time I came—weather permitting. It's supposed to be clear tomorrow, so after you finish your chores, we can go."

"That'll be afternoon," Trevor complained.

"Probably. Did you have other plans?" Lucas asked with a smile.

Jerry, the oldest of the boys, said, "Don't mind him. He's just mad 'cause he couldn't stay longer with his mom tonight. She got a job and had to work."

"You don't know nothin'," Trevor snapped and headed for the stairs.

"Trevor…" Mim called.

"I'll go talk to him," Lucas offered.

After Wyatt and his wife exchanged a look, she nodded.

Olivia felt awkward as Lucas climbed the wooden staircase. The three boys were studying her curiously.

"A fine welcome this is," Wyatt mumbled. "C'mon, Olivia. Take that coat off. Your hands were cold. We'll build a fire and get you warmed up while the boys help Mim get supper on the table."

Mim patted her shoulder. "We really are glad you came. Make yourself at home."

As Olivia shrugged out of her jacket, she realized that this looked exactly like a home should. The long couch in tones of red, navy and deep green, with its thunderbird design, looked comfortable. The scatter rugs on the hardwood floor carried various colors with Native American patterns. Two other chairs, one a recliner, one a rocker, sat at angles to the sofa. All the furniture was grouped around a slate rock fireplace and chimney that added more texture and natural color to the room.

"I hope you can forgive Trevor's rudeness," Wyatt said as he moved the black fire screen. "I don't know if Lucas told you anything about the boys…"

She crossed to the fireplace and laid her jacket

across the rocker. "He told me about their backgrounds."

"Did he mention he and Trevor have formed some kind of bond?"

She shook her head.

"Trevor was really having a tough time before Lucas's last visit. But he took the boy out riding, and when they came back, something was different. And since then, Trevor hasn't been quite as fractious."

There had been a note that had characterized Lucas's voice when he'd talked about Trevor. She'd love to go upstairs and listen in on the conversation, but she knew she couldn't.

Wyatt took two logs from the holder on the hearth and positioned them on the kindling. "How are you feeling? Lucas told us you were having a problem with morning sickness."

"It's been better," Olivia murmured, wondering just what else Lucas had told them.

Straightening, Wyatt picked up a metal box from the mantel and took off the lid. "Lucas explained what happened, Olivia, and that you're staying with him."

She couldn't help the blush that rushed to her cheeks. "We're trying to get to know each other."

With a wry grin Wyatt picked a match from the box. "How's it going?"

Olivia got the feeling that honesty was important in this home. "Sometimes good. Sometimes awkward."

"But there's a chance for the two of you?"

When she thought about Lucas and his kisses, about his tender care of her and her growing feelings for him, she answered, "There's definitely a chance."

"Don't let the boy steamroll you. He can be head-strong and stubborn." Wyatt paused. "But he has a good heart."

"There are tons of questions I'd like to ask you. But I know I have to learn about Lucas from Lucas."

"You're a wise young lady." Striking the match, Wyatt lit the kindling under the logs.

A warmth glowed in Olivia's heart because she felt she had just earned a very important seal of approval. "Maybe I should see if your wife needs help in the kitchen."

After he positioned the fire screen in place, Wyatt sat on the rocker and motioned to the chair. "She and the boys have their routine down to a science. Stay and chat with me a while."

About fifteen minutes later, Mim beckoned to them. Wyatt suggested, "Go on in. I'll call Lucas and Trevor."

As Olivia crossed to the kitchen, she realized how much she liked Wyatt. They'd talked about Flagstaff and the differences between living here rather than in Phoenix, how the Phoenix area attracted retirees but how Flagstaff attracted tourists on their way to the Grand Canyon. She'd also learned the addition to the side of the house was Wyatt's office. He was an ac-countant as well as a rancher.

Olivia pushed open the swinging door into the kitchen and found a large dining room along with the more functional area with appliances. The cupboards were knotty pine, the counters a soft blue. A long trestle table sat on blue-and-white vinyl flooring and the blue gingham curtains and appliance covers added to the homey feel.

"C'mon in," Mim said with a smile as she carried

a huge bowl of mashed potatoes to the table. "Jerry will show you your place."

Seated between five-year-old Russ and seven-year-old Kurt, Olivia smiled at Lucas as he and Trevor took their seats. He arched a brow, but his expression was still serious. She wondered if his somberness had to do with her or with his talk with Trevor.

Conversation flowed as Mim passed a platter of roasted chicken from the lazy Susan in the middle of the table. Glasses of milk sat at all the places, even Lucas's, and Olivia had to smile.

Wyatt was talking to Lucas about the price of feed when Russ reached for his glass of milk. It tipped, clattered against Olivia's, and both spilled across the table and onto her jeans. She hopped up and grabbed her napkin but not before most of it dripped onto her legs.

Jumping off his chair, Russ stared at her with wide green eyes. "I'm sorry. I didn't mean it. Don't be mad." His voice sounded as if he was ready to cry, and she thought she heard fear. This was the little boy who had been abused, and she imagined it had happened for much less than spilled milk.

Everyone around the table was silent.

"I'm not mad," she said keeping her voice gentle. "Grab your napkin and help me catch it."

Russ just gaped at her for a moment, then moved to her side. As they saw the uselessness of their efforts, Mim brought them towels. In a few moments the table and floor were wiped clean.

"Your jeans are all wet," Jerry noted, as if she wasn't aware of the cold material on her thighs.

By her side, Russ stared up at her. With a worried look still in his eyes, he said again, "I'm sorry."

She crouched down to be at his eye level. "It's okay, Russ. Jeans wash really well. The more they're washed, the softer they get. Now why don't you sit down and finish your supper before it gets cold. I'll go change and be right back."

Russ gave her an uncertain smile then slid onto his chair.

Pushing back his, Lucas stood. "I'll get your suitcase from the Jeep."

"You're in the second room on the right upstairs. Bring the jeans down and I'll throw them in the washer," Mim offered.

As Lucas went outside, Olivia climbed the stairs, admiring the multigrained banister and wood trim. The door to her bedroom was open and she glimpsed an iron bedstead and a patchwork quilt.

A few moments later, Lucas appeared with her suitcase and lifted it to the bed. "Did you bring another pair of jeans?"

"I don't travel quite as light as you do," she teased. He hadn't even brought a duffel bag.

"I keep clothes here. It's convenient." He turned to leave but stopped at the door. "Thanks for taking it easy on Russ."

"Taking it easy? I imagine kids spill things a lot. And track mud into the house. And argue about bedtime. I'd better get used to it." She studied Lucas's face. "He was afraid I was going to hit him, wasn't he?"

"Russ wasn't used to kindness before he came here. His father either hit or shouted, and he still expects that, especially from strangers."

"Well, he won't get either from me. Don't you know that?"

"Sometimes you don't know how a person will act until they're faced with the situation," he said non-committally.

Suddenly she understood that this weekend was much more than a visit to his childhood home. "Did you bring me here to include me in your life or to see if I passed some kind of test?"

After a short silence, he answered, "Both."

She should have known to expect honesty from him, but she still felt hurt that he thought she needed a test. "I see."

"Olivia…"

"It's okay, Lucas. But now I'll know to watch my step the rest of the weekend. You'd better go back down before they wonder what we're doing."

"Not a whole lot," he muttered with a scowl, and left the room.

She felt like throwing something…or crying. Hormones again.

After dessert, Olivia insisted on helping Mim clean up the kitchen so the boys could spend time with Lucas. As she cleared the table, she wondered if she'd offered in order to earn brownie points or if she would have offered anyway *before* her conversation with Lucas. Darn him. He had her second-guessing herself.

While she and Mim worked together, Mim probed gently into her background, and Olivia didn't mind. She asked questions, too, not about Lucas specifically but about this couple who had taken him in. She learned the ranch had been in Wyatt's family for generations, and Mim couldn't have children of their own. So they took in others who need shelter and kindness for a while.

The scene in the living room when Olivia had finished helping Mim stopped her in the kitchen doorway. Lucas, Trevor, Kurt and Jerry were sprawled on the floor in front of the fire playing dominoes. Wyatt held Russ on his lap and was reading him a story. A log popped in the grate sending up a leap of sparks.

All her life, Olivia had wished for a brother or sister. As she'd grown older and realized her mother didn't intend to marry again, she'd known she would never have either. She loved her mother dearly, but always dreamed of belonging to a large family. Watching the boys interact with Lucas and Wyatt, she understood that they had those kinds of bonds here even though they weren't related by blood.

When Wyatt closed the book, he said to Russ, "Bedtime for you and Kurt."

Russ saw her, slid off of Wyatt's lap and came to her side. "You wanna see my trucks?"

"Why would she want to see your trucks? Ya only got two." Trevor shook his head. "What a baby."

Olivia understood that children craved attention. Russ was getting his in his own way, Trevor in another. "I bet Russ likes his trucks better than any of his other toys. Don't you have something you treasure more than anything else?" she asked Trevor.

"I got marbles," he mumbled.

"Any cat-eyes?"

He looked surprised she knew about marbles. "Some."

Russ tugged on her hand. "You gonna come?"

She smiled down at him. "Sure, I will."

As he led her up the steps, she felt Lucas's gaze on her back.

* * *

After all of the boys were tucked in for the night, Mim fixed herself and Olivia a cup of tea while Lucas and Wyatt drank another cup of coffee. Lucas had trouble keeping his mind on the subjects they discussed, rather than on Olivia. As a lull in the conversation enveloped them, Mim and Wyatt exchanged a look and stood.

Mim said, ''Lucas, I left extra pillows and a blanket in the laundry room.''

Wyatt curved his arm around his wife's shoulders. ''He knows how to take care of himself, hon. G'night you two. We'll see you in the morning.''

Lucas watched the two people he respected most in the world climb the steps together.

''Are you sleeping down here?'' Olivia asked from her end of the sofa.

Chagrined by the way he'd handled Olivia earlier, he realized there wasn't only the two feet of cushion between them. ''The sofa opens into a bed.''

Her gaze collided with his. After a long moment, she cleared her throat. ''I'd better turn in, too.''

Before she moved even farther away, and it had seemed as if the distance between them had increased as the night had worn on, he confessed, ''I was concerned about this weekend, Olivia. I didn't know how you'd take to all this.''

''You mean the boys.''

''And Mim and Wyatt. A more rustic life.''

''Just because I don't own a pair of boots doesn't mean I can't enjoy life on a ranch.''

''You haven't seen much yet.''

''I'm hoping you'll show me around tomorrow.''

Her green eyes were guileless, and he suddenly realized she really was comfortable here. "I'll put it first on my schedule."

She smiled and her voice went softer. "I'd like that."

Frustrated with putting his desire on the back burner, he closed the gap between them until their knees touched. "I know you have to make up your own mind about working during your pregnancy and what you'll do afterward. How you want to raise our child. But you've got to understand that sometimes I feel as if I'm on the outside looking in, and all I can do is tell you what I think is best."

She laid her hand on his thigh. "I want to know what you think is best. But you have to understand becoming a mother is new to me, too, and I need time to weigh all my thoughts before I make decisions."

Her hand on his thigh created the need for more touch rather than distance. "I'm trying to give you time."

"I know you are," she said softly.

The whole world seemed to still as he bent his head and she leaned toward him. Their lips met for a brief instant before he opened his mouth over hers. He was hungry for her, had been since Christmas Eve. Lips on lips...tongue stroking tongue...weren't nearly enough. For Olivia, either, because her arms wrapped around him to pull him closer. Her sweater met his shirt and he could feel her breasts, the difference in them that had happened gradually over the past few weeks.

He wanted to see them, touch them, taste them. Her breath became his, and he lay back on the sofa pulling her on top of him. His senses were alert to the low murmur in her throat, the more fervent grasp of her hand on his shoulder, the softness of her fingertips on his neck, the floral scent that always clung to her hair. Her slender legs were erotic against his, the weight of her a sweet pleasure.

Stroking down her back, his hands cupped her buttocks. When his arousal pressed against her, she moved over him, and he wondered if she knew what she was doing to him.

He ended the kiss to move his lips along her cheek, down her neck. As she murmured his name, he pushed up against her, seeking pleasure while giving it.

With a groan he asked, "Olivia? Do you know how much I've wanted this? How much I want you?"

When Olivia stilled, he knew he had broken the spell. She was going to think instead of acting on impulse and that meant—

"Lucas. We can't do this. The boys and Mim and Wyatt…"

She tried to get up but he held her to him. "Kiss me good-night, Olivia. Show me that you want more than sleeping in separate bedrooms."

When she hesitated, he muttered, "Never mind." He couldn't believe he had asked for a woman to kiss him. Male pride made him shift his legs out from under hers. Sitting up, he stared straight ahead into the dying fire and took a few deep breaths.

"Lucas, it's not that—"

"I know what it is," he cut in, not wanting a discussion about her lack of desire for him. Obviously need didn't surge through her whenever they were near each other.

The expression on Lucas's face, along with his rigid body language told Olivia not to touch him, maybe not to even talk to him. She'd *wanted* to kiss him, but she'd known if she had, she'd be committing herself to him in more than a physical way. She simply wasn't ready for that. "I'm going to turn in," she said.

He still stared straight ahead.

"I'm sorry."

"There's nothing to be sorry about," he returned sharply. "I thought there was a fire between us but apparently I'm the only one feeling it."

"That's not true. But I *am* the one who's pregnant, and I don't think you have any idea how difficult it is sorting everything out."

"'Everything' meaning…"

"What this pregnancy means to my life."

"Well, when you figure it out, be sure to let me know."

"Wyatt said you could be headstrong and stubborn. He forgot to mention exasperating!"

At Lucas's lack of response, she rolled her eyes and headed for the steps. But suddenly she realized Lucas had told her what he was feeling, even if it was only desire. They were finally really getting to know each other.

Despite her frustration with his present attitude, she had to smile. Whether Lucas Hunter knew it or not, he was letting his guard down. That realization gave her hope.

Chapter Seven

Morning on the ranch was a whirlwind of activity, from a breakfast of eggs, sausage and pancakes to the chores that taught the boys about responsibility and working together. Mim let Olivia help with breakfast, but insisted her guest should relax and enjoy herself. Lucas found her a pair of boots and took her on a brief tour. Someone was always out and about or nearby, and they didn't have any time alone. But Lucas's remote attitude didn't invite conversation, either.

He watched her closely as he showed her around the barn, and she didn't understand why. Though she'd never been around horses, she enjoyed their beauty and wanted to get as close as she could. Bullet's muzzle against her neck and jacket didn't bother her in the least. As she stroked the horse's nose, and watched the pregnant mare farther up the row of stalls, she marveled at the idea a foal would be born to Night Song soon. In fact after examining the mare,

Lucas seemed to think she'd foal in the next twenty-four hours.

Olivia marveled at the idea that she herself would be giving birth at the end of September. When Lucas's gaze locked to hers over Night Song, she realized he was thinking the same thing. But before either of them could voice their thoughts, Russ came rushing in with a broom to sweep the walkway down the center of the barn. All the boys were anxious to complete their chores so they could go riding with Lucas after lunch.

As Mim served hot bowls of soup and homemade bread, Trevor cocked his head and asked Olivia, "Are you comin' riding?"

She'd heard that pregnant women still rode if it was part of their normal routine. But since she'd never ridden... "Not this time."

Trevor looked satisfied that they'd have Lucas to themselves.

When the men and boys left the kitchen, Olivia stood to help Mim clear the table. But she suddenly felt very tired as she carried bowls to the sink.

"Lucas is more quiet than usual this weekend," Mim observed.

Olivia met Mim's gaze and realized she could confide in her. "We have a lot of things to work out, but I didn't realize a visit here would be one of them. He's watching me as if he expects me to suddenly demand he take me home. I don't understand it."

"You're seeing each other in a different environment."

The observation was accurate but didn't satisfy her. "It's more than that. It's as if he expects me to *not* like being around the boys, to find fault— Oh, I don't know. Maybe my imagination is working overtime.''

"Or your intuition."

"You know what's bothering him, don't you?" Olivia asked, sure that something was.

Mim gathered the silverware from the table. "Has Lucas told you about Celeste?"

"Celeste? Is this someone he…dated?''

"She wanted to marry Lucas. For all the wrong reasons. And he was smitten with her until they spent a weekend here."

"She didn't like it here?"

"That's putting it mildly.''

"And if I ask Lucas about it?''

"He won't want to discuss it. But that's even more reason he should.''

Olivia opened the dishwasher to load it, knowing Mim was right. When she finished and straightened quickly, she felt a little woozy.

"Olivia? Are you all right?'' Mim asked, concern in her tone.

"I'm fine. The doctor told me my blood pressure's a little low and when I straighten up too fast, I get dizzy sometimes.'' But she sat at a kitchen chair to make sure the fuzziness had passed.

"The altitude here is higher than in Phoenix, and you were pretty active this morning. Drink lots of water to keep yourself hydrated.''

"I feel so silly when this happens.'' She remembered the day Lucas carried her from her office.

The kitchen work forgotten, Mim pulled out a chair and sat beside her. "Your body is going through so many changes to get you ready for this baby, you have to be kind to yourself. Why don't you go take a nap while everyone's out?''

''I'd rather stay here and help you.''

Mim patted her hand. ''You can help with supper. Go on. Give yourself a break. Think of it as storing up your energy for next week.''

Feeling close to Mim already, Olivia said what she was thinking. ''Lucas was very fortunate to have you and Wyatt while he was growing up.''

''We just tried to do our best. You and Lucas will do the same.''

A few minutes later, as Olivia undressed, slipped on her nightgown and settled herself under the bed quilt, she hoped Mim was right.

Snuggling into the pillow, she closed her eyes wondering just who Celeste was and what she looked like.

When Lucas quietly opened the door to the guest room, late-afternoon light streamed from the window across the foot of the bed. Olivia was curled on her side facing him, but apparently she hadn't heard the door open because her eyes remained closed. She'd tucked her right hand under her cheek. With her auburn hair streaming across the flannel pillowcase, she looked as pale as the moon, and as beautiful.

He thought about last night on the sofa. After she'd told him how exasperating he was and gone to bed, he'd realized something. She wouldn't let them satisfy their desire unless she decided to marry him! Sitting alone in front of the fire last night, aching for her, he knew she wasn't being coy. After all, she'd told him why she'd still been a virgin. In her mind, having a physical relationship with a man meant being committed to him.

He'd hoped this weekend would give them both some answers about where they were headed, but the future seemed even more muddled, and he couldn't help but worry she was holding back because of Whitcomb. She'd seemed to accept what the ranch meant to him as well as his background, without either disturbing her. But was she comparing him to another man who didn't have the baggage Lucas did?

As if Olivia sensed his silent regard, she opened her eyes.

Crossing to the bed, he sat on the edge. "Mim said you were dizzy."

She combed her hair away from her forehead and propped up against the pillow and the headboard. "I feel much better now."

He couldn't keep his gaze from lingering on her bare arms, her breasts rising and falling. He watched her nipples harden under the silky fabric and his eyes lifted to hers. There was desire there, the same desire he felt. He was sure of it. But apparently it wasn't enough. Standing, he knew he had to leave.

"Lucas, tell me about Celeste."

A cold wind swept across his heart. "There's nothing to tell."

"Mim said—"

He frowned. "I didn't think Mim would speak out of turn."

"She didn't. She just said Celeste wanted to marry you, and you brought her here."

"It didn't work out. End of story."

"I don't think so."

And Olivia thought *he* could be exasperating? "It's in the past, Olivia. Let's leave it there."

"Your past is as much a part of you as this ranch.

You keep a lot of it hidden, Lucas. I'd like to know why.''

"Maybe you don't have a right to know why,'' he replied sharply.

Her silence magnified the hurt in her green eyes. And he didn't know why he'd been harsh when what he really wanted—

"Lucas!'' a voice called from the stairs as at least two pairs of feet thumped on the wooden treads.

As Olivia pulled the quilt up to her shoulders, he crossed to the door. "I'm coming,'' he called into the hall, then he turned toward her again. "I told them I'd help put together a model airplane.''

"And I told Mim I'd help her with supper. I'd better get dressed.''

But she didn't move from the bed, and he knew that she wouldn't as long as he was in the room. His voice was gruff as he said, "I'll see you downstairs.''

She didn't respond, and he knew he'd put more distance between them again instead of solidifying the thready bond that had developed since Christmas Eve.

A snowball whizzed by the back porch as Olivia stepped outside on Sunday afternoon. She blinked her eyes against the sunlight glistening and melting the fields layered in white. Lucas, Russ and Jerry were building a snowman while Kurt and Trevor were pelting each other with snowballs.

Jerry called to her. "Are you going to help?''

She'd borrowed gloves as well as boots from Mim, hoping she could join in. But she wouldn't unless the boys wanted her there. "If you'd like. I thought this might be an all-guys project.'' Her gaze locked to Trevor's.

"You can help if you want," he mumbled grudgingly.

The snow swallowed her boots as she made her way over to Lucas.

"What time do you want to leave?" he asked as Jerry helped Russ roll a second ball of snow.

"That's what I wanted to ask you." There had been a strained tension between them ever since yesterday when he'd told her she had no right to ask questions about his life. Last night she'd gone to bed at the same time as Mim and Wyatt, deciding to give herself and Lucas some space.

"If you want to leave, we can go when we're finished with this," he said.

"If we stay, Mim said she'd show me how to crochet a sweater for the baby, and we can have an early supper. She made apple pies."

He smiled. "She knows I'll postpone leaving for a piece of her pie. Do you want to learn how to crochet?"

"I'd like to know how to make something special for the baby."

Lucas regarded her for a few moments. "We'll leave after supper then."

With Olivia helping, the snowman took shape quickly. They ended up making another and decorating both with small stones for mouths, large stones for the eyes, branches for arms and carrots for noses. Afterward, she went inside to discover the art of crocheting while Lucas and the boys played tag in the snow.

Wyatt came in from the barn before supper and announced, "Night Song's going to deliver by morning."

Olivia had never witnessed anything being born. "Really?"

"If I had to lay money on it, I'd say it'll happen around midnight," he said with a grin. "Too bad you won't be here."

Olivia glanced at Lucas who had taken his seat at the table.

His brows arched. "What? Do you want to stay?"

"Can we? I'd love to watch."

"Me, too," all the boys chimed in except for Trevor.

"Night Song's not going to want a bunch of company," Wyatt explained. "But I can wake you when she's almost ready. This might be worth missing a bit of sleep."

"I ain't goin' out to that cold barn in the middle of the night," Trevor grumbled.

"You don't have to," Mim assured him. "I've seen foals come into the world. I'll stay in here with you."

As Olivia sat across from Lucas at the table, he studied her pensively. "We can leave early tomorrow morning. If you're sure that's what you want to do."

"I'm sure." Not only did she need to see this birth, but she needed to experience it with Lucas's adopted family.

After supper, Mim helped the boys get ready for school the next day while Lucas and Wyatt went to check on Night Song. Olivia helped Russ make sure he had his crayons in his backpack. But after she and Mim put the boys to bed, she felt drawn toward the mare in labor and soon slipped into the night and headed for the barn.

Taking a deep breath of crisp night air, Olivia

raised her gaze to heaven and the hundreds of stars. There was a peace here, a soul-soothing connection to Someone greater than herself that she sometimes felt in the beauty of the desert. But here, it seemed even more tangible. Maybe it was the snow-capped mountains, the towering pines, the aspen quaking in the wind. Whatever it was, she liked it.

She'd almost reached the paddock gate when she heard voices at the barn door. The high overhead floodlight on the barn's peak kept the men in shadows.

"Will you do something for me?" she heard Wyatt ask.

"Anything," Lucas responded.

"You always say that," Wyatt remarked. "And that's why I want you to draw up my will. If anything happens to me and Mim, we want you to have the ranch."

A breeze blew across the stable yard, and in the silence Olivia stuffed her hands into her pockets.

When Lucas didn't respond immediately, Wyatt turned toward the man he had raised from a boy. "As Mim and I get older, we realize that we should have adopted you ourselves instead of waiting for another family to want you. We'd like to make you trustee of this place, to keep it as a safe home for children who have nowhere to go, or to live here as you please."

"You're a generous man, Wyatt. But I can't accept it."

"Don't you tell me 'no' without giving it some thought."

Olivia knew she shouldn't be listening, but couldn't help herself. Why would Lucas refuse Wyatt this? Because he didn't want the responsibility? Or because he didn't want to be tied down anywhere, not even here? This was a place he loved! But maybe he liked dropping in freely. On *his* terms.

If that was so, how could she ever count on him if he didn't want to be tied down?

She took a step back and her boots crunched on the snow. Lucas moved toward the gate and caught sight of her in the beam of the white floodlight.

Walking up to the gate, she unlatched it. "I was curious about what's happening to Night Song."

His blue gaze probed hers. "She's restless and only wants Wyatt nearby. But we can watch from a distance if we're quiet. Horses can delay delivery if there's too much commotion."

"I'd like to watch," Olivia answered.

Wyatt opened the barn door and Lucas waited for her to precede him inside.

At the far end of the walkway, Night Song restlessly paced and shifted in the breadth of two stalls. Apparently Lucas and Wyatt had removed a partition to make a single into a double so the mare had plenty of space. Lucas stacked bales of hay in an empty stall so Olivia could sit and watch. Leaning close to her, his breath warm on her cheek, he murmured that he and Wyatt would be in the tack room.

As the time passed, Night Song became more restless and often kicked up her legs at her belly. When Lucas returned to the barn, he saw Olivia still keeping watch over the mare. But the dampness had seeped through her and she had her arms wrapped around her.

"Cold?" he asked.

"A little."

He kept his voice low. "Do you want to go back to the house?"

She shook her head.

Nodding to another vacant stall beyond Bullet's, he crossed to it. "Let's get you warmed up a little, or else you'll catch a chill till this is over."

Not sure what he had in mind, she followed him to a stall layered with fresh hay.

"I'll be right back," he said.

In a few minutes he returned with saddle blankets. At the other end of the barn now, he spread one out over the hay and kept his voice low. "We can combine our body heat and get some rest at the same time." In a flash he'd settled on the blanket and held out his arm to her.

He was wearing an insulated plaid vest over his navy flannel shirt. He hadn't shaved since morning and light brown stubble shadowed his jaw. With him looking so ruggedly sexy, just the thought of combined body heat was enough to warm her. Besides that, there was something about Lucas's expression that urged her to take him up on his offer. They hadn't had any time to themselves since he'd left her room yesterday afternoon. Maybe space wasn't such a good idea.

As she settled in beside him, he curved his arm around her above her shoulders. With her elbow against his ribs and his jean-clad leg lodged against hers, she didn't need another blanket.

But he settled one over them. "I'm sorry about what I said yesterday."

The apology seemed difficult for him. "Did you mean what you said?" she asked softly as she stared straight ahead.

There was a pause. "I did at the time. I'm not used to anyone asking personal questions."

"Wyatt and Mim don't ask?"

"They wait and eventually I tell them."

"Do I have to wait?"

She felt his sigh and realized she'd pushed him into another corner. But they had to hash this out. "You weren't eager to tell me about the ranch, and all weekend I've gotten the feeling you expect me to turn tail and run. I'd like to know why."

At his silence, she leaned away slightly so she could gauge his expression. The nerve in his jaw worked and she knew she had to do something to break through his barricades. She gently laid her hand on his arm. "Lucas?"

His muscles tensed under her fingers. Finally he said, "Celeste and I dated for a few months. We both had busy lives. She owned a boutique and often worked on weekends, so when I flew up here, she didn't care."

"Did she know you'd grown up on the ranch?"

"I told her before I brought her here."

This time Olivia did wait, hoping Lucas would continue without her pressing him.

In a few moments, he did. "It turned out Celeste was only interested in my image—the successful lawyer who flew his own plane, took her to expensive restaurants and cocktail parties with wealthy clients. Looking back now, I realize that's the limited view she saw of me and I didn't have a much better perspective on her. She was beautiful, cultured, from an excellent family, but I didn't realize till I brought her here that she was a snob...and not just a snob. She was a woman who didn't like being around children."

"Were you planning to marry her?" Olivia asked with a lump in her throat.

"We'd discussed it. And having children. But when we came here, I saw her turn away from Russ's tears after he'd fallen and skinned his knee. She left the room whenever more than adults were in it, and she yelled at Kurt for putting a sticky handprint on her purse. After all that, I knew she was the type of woman who would let a nanny raise her children before she sent them to boarding school."

Now Olivia understood why he'd hesitated to tell her about his background and the ranch. And if he'd truly loved this woman... But he'd never mentioned love. "I would never want a nanny to raise my child," she murmured.

"But you want to establish your career." His blue eyes examined her with an intensity that tried to see to the core of who she was.

So *that's* why he'd reacted so strongly when she'd told him about Barrington's job offer. Still, she needed him to realize she was very different from Celeste. "Lucas, I haven't thought everything out yet about the baby...and working. But I want to feed our child, and hug our child, and clean off sticky fingers along with bandaging boo-boos. Most of all, I want to rock him or her and sing lullabies. I promise you that."

The barn was rife with a heavy silence for a moment as he weighed her words. Night Song's pacing and the rustling of straw broke it. Then Lucas slid his hand under Olivia's hair and tipped her chin up with his thumb. "I believe promises are made to be kept."

"So do I," she agreed solemnly.

As he bent his head to her, Wyatt came into the barn.

Lucas's lips brushed against hers in a kiss that was frustratingly short but thoroughly sense stirring.

"You'd better nap while you can or tomorrow's going to be one very long day."

She knew he was right, and as he drew her close to his body so she could use his shoulder as a pillow, she felt so very comfortable snuggling in his arms. So comfortable that the images floating through her mind put a smile on her lips.

It seemed like only a few minutes until Wyatt called to them that Night Song was down and ready to foal. Her hand lay across Lucas's chest and his lips almost brushed her temple. When she sat up, she saw his gaze was alert.

"Did you sleep?" she asked.

"I rested," he answered with a crooked smile that melted her heart. "I'll see if Wyatt needs help with Night Song. You call the boys. This can happen fast."

Mim and Olivia bundled Kurt, Russ and Jerry into coats, hats, gloves, and boots. They'd stayed dressed instead of changing into pajamas so they'd be ready. To Olivia's surprise, Trevor, too, had remained dressed and was ready to go out to the barn with the others. When he passed by her in the kitchen, he said, "Too much noise to sleep. I'm comin', too."

The boys ran ahead to the barn. When Olivia and Mim reached the door, Lucas had corralled them and was explaining, "This isn't a circus, guys. You're going to have to stay back and keep the noise level down or you'll have to go back to the house. Understand?"

They all nodded.

Lucas led them inside, and they lined up against Night Song's stall to watch. Olivia stood behind Russ, her hands on his shoulders, as Lucas knelt beside the mare across from Wyatt.

"There's feet! I see feet!" Kurt exclaimed, then clamped his hand over his mouth.

The forefeet appeared with a contraction then disappeared when it was over. But as Night Song whinnied, straw sticking to her coat where she had sweated, another contraction hit.

"It looks like a water balloon!" Jerry said in a whisper as the forefeet and sac appeared again.

"That's sort of what it is," Lucas informed them. "It protects the foal until it's ready for the world."

Suddenly the sac broke and fluid rushed out, immediately followed by the forefeet and the nose of the foal! Not long after, the rest of the foal lay atop the straw, still attached to its mother by the umbilical cord.

"Wow!" Russ gasped, and Olivia's hands tightened on his shoulders as her eyes filled with tears.

When Lucas glanced at her, his gaze held hers for a poignant moment. She tried to blink her tears away, but his slow smile said he understood exactly how she felt. A foal. A baby. Miracles...and they were sharing the experience.

As Wyatt crooned to the mare to keep her still, Lucas explained to the boys about the cord and rubbed down the foal with a towel.

Finally the foal kicked free of the mare and the umbilical cord broke off. A short time later Night Song got to her feet and licked her baby who began trying to scramble to its feet. One, two, three tries until finally its wobbly legs supported it.

"We've got a filly," Wyatt said with a grin. "You boys will have to think of a good name for her."

The same sorrel as her mother, the filly had four white stockings and a blaze down her nose. She nuzzled her mother and began suckling.

Coming out of the stall, Lucas curved his arm around Russ. "Okay, boys. Back to the house. We'll give mother and daughter here some privacy." To Olivia he said, "Go on to bed. I'll help Wyatt finish up out here. We'll leave around five-thirty."

Olivia nodded, knowing if they both arrived at Barrington late, there might be gossip. Suddenly the thought of gossip didn't seem so daunting. Whether it had happened this weekend or before, she didn't know. But she'd fallen in love with Lucas Hunter—thoroughly and irrevocably—and that disconcerted her a great deal more than the threat of a few rumors.

Because she had no idea how Lucas truly felt about her.

Smothering a yawn, Olivia picked up the phone at her desk Monday afternoon when it buzzed.

"Olivia, it's me."

She smiled as Lucas's voice reminded her of their weekend, their drive back to Scottsdale this morning and their mad dash to get to work on time. They'd driven in separately, not knowing what the day would bring.

"Are you going to be late tonight?" she asked, thinking about what was in the refrigerator or freezer that they could make for supper.

"I have to fly to Grand Junction, Colorado, this afternoon. I'll be in meetings tonight and tomorrow. But I should be home by supper tomorrow."

She felt deflated, as if the sun had disappeared behind a cloud. "I'll probably go home and sack out for the night. Lack of sleep is catching up with me. How about you?"

"I don't need as much sleep as you," he teased.

With June sitting a few feet away, she couldn't make a comment about her pregnancy. "Fly safely," she said instead, wanting to run to his office down the hall and give him a hug before he left, but not feeling free enough with him to do that.

His deep voice was sure. "I always do. See you tomorrow."

After Olivia hung up, she noticed June giving her a curious glance...and wondered if it showed that she was already missing Lucas.

Checking her watch for at least the hundredth time Tuesday evening, Olivia switched on the television. Lucas hadn't come home and he hadn't called. She didn't even have any idea where he was staying in Grand Junction! She could call Rex Barrington....

Oh, Lucas would love it if she checked up on him. Maybe he had decided to spend another night in Colorado.

Then why hadn't he called?

Crossing to the kitchen, she switched off the oven. The turkey breast was well past done. The baked potatoes had fared better. Not that it mattered. She wasn't the least bit hungry. If Lucas didn't walk in that door by 10:00 p.m., she'd call Rex Barrington and the consequences be damned.

Her hands shook as she stowed the food in the refrigerator and cleaned every surface in the kitchen to give herself something physical to do.

At 9:45 the lock on the front door turned and Lucas's footsteps sounded in the foyer. She told herself to stay calm, not overreact, give him a chance to explain. Trying to swallow the lump in her throat and the urge to cry, she took a deep breath and hurried to the living room.

When he saw her, he dropped his suitcase by the sofa. "I had a delay taking off at the airport, and then I had to fly around some storm cells. I would have just put down somewhere, but I wanted to get back tonight. I hope you didn't worry."

He hoped she hadn't worried?

She remembered when she'd come home late. Had he felt what she was feeling now? The absolute relief? Anxiety from the last few hours bubbled up and spilled out. "I *was* worried. I didn't have any idea where you were staying in Grand Junction, if you'd left, if you'd crashed…"

Her love for Lucas had become too deep for her to ignore, too wide to detour, too intense for her to take the safe road any longer. She wanted to *have* rights where Lucas Hunter was concerned, and she wanted to get much closer than merely being housemates would allow.

Taking another deep breath, she decided her future. "If your proposal still stands, Lucas, I'm ready to marry you."

Chapter Eight

Lucas's heart pounded, and he forgot he was tired from a day full of meetings, let alone flying around storm cells that made him wonder more than once if he was crazy to be out there. All he could think about was getting home to Olivia....

And now here she was, standing in front of him looking beautifully ruffled, not angry because he was late but wanting to marry him.

"Do you mean that?" he asked, wondering why she had made the decision, but glad she had.

She nodded...slowly, as if she was just realizing the impact of what she'd said.

In a stride and a half he was close enough to kiss her, but wasn't sure that's what he should do. He hated feeling unsure. But ever since Christmas Eve, the direction he should follow with Olivia was foggy.

"What made you decide?" He wasn't exactly certain what he was hoping she'd answer.

Her cheeks flushed as they often did when he put

her on the spot. "I...uh...I just realized if something happened to you, I'd have no proof you were the father. I want our baby to know who his father is. I want him to have two parents under the same roof who are more than...housemates."

Some of the lightness left Lucas because he believed what Olivia couldn't put into words was more basic than his name on the birth certificate. She wanted security for her child. Without marriage she didn't believe she had it. *With* marriage it was guaranteed. This was as practical a decision on her part as his proposal had been to begin with. "Let's fly to Las Vegas this weekend."

"This weekend?"

"The sooner we're married, the sooner we can stop pretending we're mere acquaintances and tell the world about your pregnancy."

"Oh, but we can't say anything right away. Everyone will know..."

"That we couldn't resist each other?" he asked gruffly. Olivia was still worried about what her colleagues at Barrington thought—maybe one man in particular.

"Maybe it's not important to you, Lucas, and maybe people will count the months after the baby's born, but I'd like everyone to get used to the fact we're married before we announce that I'm pregnant."

It was a small request, really. As long as they were getting married and he could tell everyone, including Stanley Whitcomb, that Olivia was his, he could wait on announcing that he was going to become a father. "We'll give it a few weeks. But it's all the more reason to get married sooner rather than later."

After studying him for a few moments, she agreed, "All right. This weekend."

"You won't be sorry, Olivia. I'll take care of all the arrangements. We'll book a flight on a jet so you don't have to worry about flying...or anything else."

"I never imagined getting married without my mother."

The wistfulness in her voice made him suggest, "We can fly her in."

"You mean that?"

He'd fly in anybody she wanted, just for another one of those smiles! "Sure. What about your dad?"

She hesitated. "I...uh...don't know how to reach him. He travels a lot."

They'd never really discussed her father. When she'd told him about her parent's divorce, she'd only talked about her childhood with her mother. "Maybe your mother does."

Olivia shook her head. "She doesn't. Are you going to ask Mim and Wyatt?"

"I'd like them there, but they'll have trouble getting away from the ranch and the boys. And it's tax season for Wyatt."

"But you'll ask?"

"No. I don't want to put them on the spot. We'll call after we're married and drive up there after we get back."

"You're sure?"

For a moment he wasn't, but he didn't like asking Mim and Wyatt for more than they'd already given him. "I'm sure. Why don't you call your mother? Then I'll try to get some reservations set up."

Unable to keep from touching Olivia any longer, his whole body thrumming with the knowledge she would soon be his, he brushed her hair behind her ear. "We'll make this work, Olivia, if we both want it."

She nodded, but he thought he saw doubts in her eyes. Bending to kiss her, he was determined to make those doubts vanish…if not before the wedding, then definitely during their honeymoon. Respecting her wishes, he'd wait to take her to his bed until after the ceremony. But then she'd see that they belonged together. Then she'd see that her future was with him.

Checking her watch, Olivia closed the manila folder and stacked it with others on her desk. She'd asked Stanley if she could leave early today for the weekend. He'd had no objections. This morning she'd agreed to meet Lucas at his office at one o'clock. They were flying to Las Vegas this afternoon and getting married tomorrow afternoon.

Her heart thumped just thinking about it, let alone doing it. Since Lucas had returned home from Grand Junction, they'd made plans. Her mother had taken the day off to fly to Vegas and insisted on making reservations for dinner as a precelebration. Olivia had bought a new dress for the occasion since she'd decided to wear her ivory suit for the wedding. After all, she'd only worn it once before, for the office Christmas party! She'd also bought a new nightgown and robe in an aqua silk.…

Lucas had kissed her Tuesday night—a kiss that could have taken them to bed. But then he'd backed off, and she guessed it was a strategy to increase their anticipation for their wedding night. She wished he'd tell her what he was feeling. Since last weekend at the ranch and learning about his experience with Celeste, she understood him much better. And she loved him, enough to marry him without knowing what he felt for her.

"Olivia, I know you said you want to leave by one, but can I speak to you for a few minutes?" Stanley asked from his office doorway.

June hadn't returned from lunch, and Olivia knew Lucas was probably waiting to leave. But she wasn't prepared to tell Stanley why she was ready to dash out the door. After all he'd done for her, she could certainly give him a few minutes. She and Lucas had time until their flight left.

While she sat in the chair in front of his desk, her boss lodged a hip on a corner. "As you know, I have a daughter in college."

Stanley spoke of his offspring proudly. She'd been valedictorian of her high school graduating class. "How is she?"

"Well, that's the problem. She thinks she's fine. I think she's crazy!" Stanley looked worried and upset.

"What happened?"

"She called me this morning. She wants to quit college and get married! Her boyfriend's in med school and she wants to go to work and help put him through. I couldn't convince her she needs her degree as much as he does. You're close to her age. I wondered if you could help me with some convincing arguments to change her mind."

Stanley's words—*you're close to her age*—brought home a truth Olivia should have realized before today. He thought of her in the same way he thought of his daughter—fondly, with a protective care she'd always wanted from her father. Only, he'd never been around to give it. When she'd come to work at Barrington under Stanley's supervision, he'd filled that gap. There had never been anything more.

She thought about her feelings for Lucas that had deepened over the past month. "I don't know how I can help you, Stanley. Because if she really loves this man, you won't be able to change her mind. It might be best if you talk to both of them about this. Find out exactly what they're going to do. Get a sense of whether he's taking advantage of her, or if this will be a joint effort and he'll support her when she does want to go back to school."

"So you think if I oppose this marriage, she'll do what she wants anyway?"

"Didn't you tell me she has a mind of her own?"

He shook his head. "I don't want her to make a mistake she'll regret."

"All you can do is talk to her and then be there for her if she needs you."

As Stanley studied Olivia, a slow smile curved his lips. "You didn't give me what I wanted."

"What did you want?"

"Ammunition to change her mind."

"I'll bet she knows—just as well as you do—all the reasons she should get her degree."

After a pause, he stood and so did she. Then he laid his hand on her shoulder. "Thank you for giving me some perspective."

She smiled. "It's much easier when it's not *my* life."

Opening the door to Whitcomb's office suite, Lucas saw that Olivia's desk chair was vacant. But he heard voices and spotted her in Whitcomb's office. Her boss had left the door open. His gut clenched when he realized they were engrossed in conversation, gazing into each other's eyes. Frozen, he watched, only hearing the murmur of their words, not the content.

When Stanley Whitcomb stood and Olivia did, too, he almost expected...

Whitcomb's hand on Olivia's shoulder pushed Lucas to move forward and make his presence known before he saw his intended wife in Whitcomb's arms...before...

Olivia turned and her gaze lifted to his face.

"Are you ready?" he asked, his voice curt.

Dropping his hand to his side, Stanley answered, "We're just finishing up. Olivia didn't mention she was meeting *you*."

Olivia blushed, and he wanted to shout that they were flying off to get married. But Lucas held back, suddenly wondering if she'd changed her mind. "We have plans for the weekend," he answered, not caring if Olivia objected.

Stanley's brows arched. "Well...then I'll see you Monday morning, Olivia. Enjoy your weekend."

After she said goodbye to Stanley, her glare at Lucas was self-explanatory and her silence on the way to the parking lot told him she was either upset or angry.

Once they were seated in his Jeep, he asked, "Are we still getting married?"

"Why are you asking?"

He hated when she answered his question with a question. But it was a tactic he knew well. "I want you to be sure."

"I *am* sure, Lucas. But if you have doubts..."

He had doubts, all right. Not about marrying her, but about leftover feelings she might harbor for Whitcomb. Switching on the ignition, he said, "I'm ready to do this. We forgot to buy wedding rings. Maybe we'll have time to get them before we meet your mother."

Olivia didn't respond, but fastened her seat belt.

He had the feeling this was going to be a very long night.

When the bellboy opened the hotel room door, Olivia crossed the threshold first and took a breath at what she saw. Two steps down from the entranceway would take her to the sitting area with its fireplace, sofa, chair and entertainment center. The mint-green carpet coordinated with the mauve and green fabrics covering the furniture. Her gaze passed from the sofa, up three steps to the white wrought-iron railing and the immense round bed beyond. A mirror on the light oak dresser reflected the draperies closed over an expansive picture window.

Lucas had tipped the bellboy and closed the door when Olivia turned toward him. He'd tugged off his tie and rolled up his white shirtsleeves at the airport before they'd taken off. His mood had been remote since he'd found her talking to Stanley, and she wasn't sure if he was angry because she'd been late or because he was jealous. And if he was jealous, nothing she could say would help. Even if she told him she loved him...

She suspected Lucas didn't put much store in the words or maybe even the feeling. When he'd first asked her to marry him, he'd said, *An alliance with that fire behind it has a better chance than any romantic illusion you might favor.*

By romantic illusion, he'd meant love. No words

could convince him to believe in love. But she was hoping her actions could.

"What do you think?" he asked.

"It's...sumptuous."

He shrugged. "I wanted us to be comfortable. Your mother, too. Her room isn't as large, but I'm hoping it's just as nice. Are you going to call her?"

When they'd checked in, Olivia had asked about her mother and found she'd arrived earlier. Olivia was eager for Lucas and her mom to meet. "She said she was going to scout around for a restaurant when she arrived. I'll find out if she made reservations for dinner."

Before she went to the sitting area's phone, her gaze again went to the large round bed. She didn't know what Lucas was expecting. If they'd start their honeymoon tonight...

As if he was reading her thoughts, he said, "I can sleep on the couch tonight if you'd like. But come tomorrow, I expect to be sharing that bed. I'm not just marrying you because you're carrying my child. I expect to be a husband in every sense of the word." Turning toward the door, he opened it. "I'm going for a walk. I won't be gone long."

And before she had a chance to blink, let alone respond, the door closed behind him.

Surprise gave way to pique as Olivia crossed to the phone. Apparently Lucas wanted a baby...and sex. He couldn't have been any clearer. Well, she wanted to make love with him, too, but she wanted a heck of a lot more. If he thought he could simply make a demand and have her meet it, he was dead wrong. Tomorrow was her wedding day and she wanted vows and dreams, a little romance and definitely a husband who wanted to share forever!

As tears pricked in her eyes, she picked up the phone. Lucas had a few things to learn about being a fiancé and especially about being a husband. She was suddenly *very* glad she'd splurged on the fuchsia dress she'd bought for tonight because that dress was going to give her the confidence she needed to make Lucas Hunter see her not as the mother of his child and not as a convenient release for his needs. He'd see her as a woman in her own right with desires and needs that *might* coincide with his.

He *expected* to share that bed tomorrow?

Well, she expected more than just having sex.

Their honeymoon was going to be a journey into love and commitment and a marriage that would last.

Soft yellow lights and sultry saxophone music spilled from the elegant rooftop dining room into the foyer area as Olivia and her mother exited one of the hotel's restaurants, Lucas behind them. "I'm so glad you could come, Mom. And dinner was wonderful. Thank you."

As Lucas came up beside them, his gaze passed over her with the same intensity with which he'd watched her all evening. It had to be the dress. The beaded halter top hugged her fuller breasts as if it had been designed to flatter her, and the full taffeta skirt brushed high above her knees. In the past week the waistband on some of her skirts had felt tight, and in a few weeks this dress might not fit again until after she had her baby. But for tonight the silver desire in Lucas's eyes filled her with the determination to make their marriage more than a practical arrangement.

Shifting his attention from Olivia, Lucas addressed her mother. "Let me add my thanks to Olivia's, Mrs. McGovern."

"It's Rosemary, Lucas. You're going to be my son-in-law tomorrow. And since you're so generously paying for everything else, dinner was the least I could do. I don't know how you managed to get a ticket for me to see Barry Manilow tomorrow night, but I'm truly looking forward to it. I just hope—" She stopped abruptly as if she'd thought better about continuing.

"Feel free to say what's on your mind...Rosemary."

"I just hope you're not going to regret getting married so quickly. Olivia's always dreamed of a satin-and-lace gown, a wedding cake and reception...."

Lucas shot a glance at Olivia and frowned.

Her dreams had changed abruptly since she'd made love with Lucas and since she'd found herself pregnant. "This seemed to be the best, Mom. Because of the baby, we didn't want to wait. Would you like to come back to our room for a bit?"

Her mother accepted the change in subject with an understanding smile and hooked her arm through Olivia's. "I'm going back to *my* room. Traveling wears me out and we have a big day tomorrow."

As they rode to her mother's floor, Lucas was silent. But when Rosemary exited the elevator, he held the door. "I ordered a limo to pick us up at twelve-thirty and take us to the chapel."

Her mother smiled at him. "You *do* think of everything. I'll meet you in the lobby. Get a good night's sleep."

Silence echoed in the elevator as Lucas and Olivia

rode to their floor, and she could feel the tension in him as they walked to their room. When he opened the door, Olivia stepped inside, remembering his return from his walk earlier. She'd already dressed; he'd stared at her as if he was seeing her for the first time. As soon as he'd showered and changed, they'd gone to the jewelry store he'd found in the gallery of shops at the hotel, and they'd bought plain gold wedding rings before meeting her mother. Tomorrow morning they would go to the courthouse and take care of the license.

Following her inside now, Lucas removed his suit coat and laid it over the chair. "*Did* you want to come to Las Vegas to get married?"

Going to him, she stood close enough to breathe in his aftershave, close enough to see the tiny nick on his chin where he'd cut himself shaving. "I wouldn't be here if I didn't want to come."

His gaze searched hers, then reaching out, he clasped her elbows to draw her closer. "You look beautiful tonight. That dress—" he took a breath "—is really something."

The desire in his eyes almost melted her, but she was determined to make their wedding night more meaningful than what had happened on his couch on Christmas Eve. "I'm glad you like it," she murmured as the touch of his hands and fingers urged her to forget about tomorrow and settle for now.

"Oh, I like it," he assured her, his voice husky.

She knew if she didn't say something soon, he'd kiss her and she'd forget about waiting a moment, let alone a night. "I think you're right about tonight," she blurted out.

He tilted his head. "Right?"

"Mmm-hmm. If we wait until tomorrow to…well, you know, really sleep together, it will make the beginning of our marriage more special. Don't you think?"

His expression was a combination of perplexed and guarded. "Special?"

"I told you I had decided when I was a teenager to wait until I was married to make love. I'd still like to…even though I did slip once. So I really appreciate you remembering that. But since I'm a lot shorter, I'll take the sofa."

"Not a chance," he muttered with a scowl.

"Lucas…"

"No way, Olivia. You take the bed. I'll be fine on the couch. I sleep in my office all the time."

"If you're sure…"

Releasing her, he stepped back. "I'm sure."

Anticipation was sweet, and just to raise the stakes a little, she rose on tiptoe, placed her hands on his shoulders and placed a lingeringly soft kiss on his cheek. "Thank you." Quickly retreating before she got caught in a web of her own making, she smiled. "Go ahead and change in the bathroom if you want. I'll wait."

His glare could have burned right through her. "Fine. I'll go first." With a yank on his tie, he headed for the dresser and his sleeping shorts. She just had to remember not to look at him when he came out of the bathroom or they'd have their honeymoon *before* their wedding.

The wedding chapel's steeple rose white against a turquoise sky. Lucas held the door as Olivia and her mother entered the vestibule. This was the first chapel he'd found that actually made appointments for weddings rather than having a waiting line. They'd had enough of a wait at the courthouse this morning.

Lucas rubbed his neck. That sofa had been damn hard. Staying away from Olivia last night had been the ultimate test of his self-control. When he'd seen her in that dress... Damn his short temper *and* his jealousy of her boss. If he hadn't offered to spend the night on the couch, he might have found satisfaction for the yearning ache that had plagued him since Christmas Eve. But he'd chosen to be a gentleman and suffered for it.

And just looking at her now...

He remembered the ivory suit. She'd been stunning in it on Christmas Eve and she was just as stunning today. The hotel florist had delivered a bouquet this morning. He'd forgotten about flowers but obviously she hadn't. Not only had she ordered a bouquet and the headpiece she wore now, but a boutonniere for him. She was a traditional woman at heart, and suddenly the gold-trimmed doors before them, the papier-mâché wedding bells hanging above, the whole neon atmosphere of Las Vegas seemed wrong. Olivia deserved a real church wedding with a gown and cake—

The doors before them opened and a woman said, ''He's ready for you now.''

Lucas spotted a couple leaving by the side door. The nature of weddings here didn't lend to permanence, and he was suddenly filled with doubts. What if Olivia couldn't forget her feelings for Whitcomb? What if a child or even their desire wasn't enough of a bond to keep them together?

But then his gaze met hers. Her smile was uncertain, and he realized he had to convince her that she belonged with him and no one else, that a child and desire were the best foundation for marriage. He curved his arm around her waist. "Ready?"

She nodded and there was determination in her eyes.

The minister was pleasant and tried to put them at ease. After he took care of the paperwork, he asked them to join him at the altar where he would begin the ceremony. Olivia handed her bouquet to her mother who was their witness. It seemed like it was only moments until the minister asked Lucas to repeat after him. As Lucas studied his bride, the tiny white lilies and wispy little flowers contrasting with her beautiful auburn hair, the deep enchanting green of her eyes, the almost unnoticeable dimple at the left corner of her mouth when she tremulously smiled, he repeated words that took on a new meaning. Honor. Cherish. Till death do us part.

When Olivia said the same words, she did so without hesitation and with a clarity that made him realize how much he respected and admired her as well as desired her. The vows and exchange of rings passed in the blink of an eye, until the minister smiled and said, "You may now kiss your bride."

As Olivia gazed up at him, he was filled with the wonder that they were married, and that she finally belonged to him. When he took her in his arms, his kiss expressed the reverence of the moment and too many hopes to count.

Finally he drew away, wanting her as a husband wanted a wife. When he gazed down at her, he thought he saw the same desire he felt, the same hopes driving his need for marriage. But he couldn't be sure.

The minister wished them good luck, and Olivia's mother hugged her daughter and then him, saying, "Welcome to our family."

His voice was husky as he murmured, "Thank you."

A few minutes later, in the limo beside him, Olivia asked her mother, "Are you sure you'll be okay on your own? We could have lunch...."

"Honey, I had a big breakfast and I'm ready to go for a swim. I'm used to being on my own. Besides, I'm sure you and Lucas have better things to do than watch over me. After all, this *is* your honeymoon." Her sly smile told Lucas she knew exactly what was on *his* mind.

He shifted on the seat, his elbow rubbing Olivia's, his knee grazing hers. His bride's face was pink. "We appreciate your wanting to give us privacy, but we don't want to desert you."

"And you won't be. If I have time before dinner and the show, I'll try the slot machines. I'm going to take advantage of everything that gorgeous hotel has to offer."

As much for his sake as Olivia's, wanting to get to know his mother-in-law better, he suggested, "Why don't we have breakfast before you leave for the airport tomorrow?" Rosemary's flight left around noon. He and Olivia weren't flying back to Phoenix until later in the day.

Olivia's mother studied him, then answered, "All right. But let's make it a *late* breakfast."

There was affectionate amusement in her voice and he decided he *really* liked Rosemary McGovern.

Back in the hotel lobby, Rosemary said, "I'm going to stop in one of the shops and buy a magazine
to read at the pool. I'll see you tomorrow." With a
wave and a smile, she left them standing by an indoor
fountain, finally alone.

Lucas suddenly felt like a teenager on his first date.
It was ridiculous. This beautiful woman by his side
was his wife and she was having his baby! But Olivia
had thrown him more than one curve in the past few
weeks so he'd better tread carefully.

"Do you want to go up to the room?" he asked.

"Do you?" she returned.

He took a deep breath and held on to his patience.
They hadn't had time for lunch before they'd left for
the chapel. "If you're hungry, we could order room
service," he suggested, avoiding a direct answer, still
trying to gauge what was on her mind.

"That sounds fine."

Did he hear relief in her voice? Would she rather
eat lunch than go to bed with him?

One step at a time, Hunter. At least get to the room.

The ride in the elevator didn't help the tension.
Olivia's perfume wound around Lucas, until each
breath made him need her more. The elevator zoomed
straight to their floor and when the doors slid open,
he stepped out. Still holding her flowers, Olivia
glanced at him, then began walking toward their
room. She stopped at their door. He opened it.

If she was hungry, he would order lunch. Going to
the coffee table, he picked up the menu. "What did
you have in mind?"

Setting her flowers on the end table, Olivia tried to
figure out what was happening between her and Lucas. They'd *never* been this awkward together. The

aftermath of their tryst on Christmas Eve had come close. But they'd gotten married for goodness' sake....

And maybe he didn't know what to do next any more than she did. Maybe he was just being a gentleman. Despite his outburst yesterday, he was trying not to push her. She almost smiled. One of them had to make this easier.

Crossing to him, she took the menu from his hand and laid it on the table. "Lucas, what do *you* want?"

His gaze dipped from her eyes to her lips then back up again. "I want to make you my wife."

"Then why don't I slip into something more comfortable?" she suggested softly. With his gaze following her, she went to the closet, pulled her new nightgown and robe from the hanger and took them into the bathroom.

When she emerged a short time later, nervous yet excited, she realized she was afraid Lucas would see the changes in her body and be put off. They were subtle but becoming more noticeable—her fuller breasts, her changing waistline. But before the anxiety could overtake the excitement, she saw him stretched out, his black silk shorts dark against the white sheets. He seemed to take up most of the immense bed.

His gaze was male and hungry as it raked over the aqua silk robe that left little to his imagination. Last night he'd been settled on the couch when she'd turned off the light and slipped under the covers. There was no slipping in quickly now as she slowly approached him and stopped at the edge of the bed.

"Olivia, do I have to be careful? Is there anything I should know?" he asked, his deep concern touching her.

She shook her head and somehow found her voice. "The doctor said intercourse can be good for me. It can help my muscles prepare…" It sounded so clinical.

The muscle in his jaw worked as he held out his hand to her. After she slipped off her robe, she placed her hand in his, and he drew her to his side. The rustle of her gown on the sheet briefly covered the sound of their breathing.

The sparks of desire in Lucas's eyes singed her as his gaze slid from the spaghetti straps, over her hips to the length of her legs. When he looked at her face again, he said, "I want you. But if you have any doubts about this…"

"This" could mean their marriage. "This" could mean making love with him. She had no doubts about either. But showing him could be more effective than trying to tell him. She remembered what he'd asked her to do in front of the fire at the ranch. With her heart pounding, she moved closer and touched her lips to his.

A shudder ran through him, and his fingers stole under her hair as he brought her close. When his mouth covered hers, she held on to him for a moment, then gave herself the freedom to enjoy…and explore. As Lucas's kiss grew urgent and possessive, her fingertips discovered again the tautness of his shoulder muscles, the heat of his skin, the strength that she knew was deeper than physical.

Lucas's tongue foraged more completely, and each stroke and thrust stoked a flame that already burned bright. She found herself starved for body contact, and she pressed against him to appease the need that was burgeoning the longer they kissed. Lucas's hands became an extension of the fire that made her gasp for air as he broke the kiss. She didn't understand why he'd separated from her, until he brushed her straps from her shoulders and stared at her breasts.

She didn't know how sensitive they'd be now, she didn't know if... Her thoughts vanished as his mouth closed over her nipple and she moaned. The sensation was heavenly. His tongue was like velvet...playing, seducing.

Somehow her gown landed on the floor next to his shorts. Somehow she forgot about the changes in her body. Somehow she got lost in Lucas.

Chapter Nine

The knowledge that Olivia was carrying his child was like an aphrodisiac Lucas didn't need. He felt as if he'd wanted her forever and needed her longer. His hands were trembling, and he tore his mouth from hers to stop the spiral of sensations he didn't understand. It seemed as if he was touching a woman for the first time, as if everything he knew about pleasure had been an illusion. When he gazed into Olivia's eyes, he saw heaven and earth and everything in between. Nothing about their first time together had prepared him for this.

The feelings shook him and the foundation of the life he'd created for himself. Olivia and their child were now the center. He kissed her neck, needing to bury his face in her hair. When he licked and toyed with her earlobe, placed an openmouthed kiss at the tender spot behind her ear, she scraped her nails down his back, and he gloried in his power to pleasure her.

"Do you know how beautiful you are, Olivia? How I've dreamed of us like this?"

"It's not a dream anymore," she whispered breathlessly as he felt her breasts against him.

He knew he had to be gentle. He'd read that women's breasts could be supersensitive during pregnancy. But her sultry voice, the sweet scent of her, her intoxicating taste fogged his thoughts until he relied on instinct rather than expertise. He drew her even closer, aroused beyond normal limits, shaking with a need that had built in him for his entire adult life.

As Olivia caressed him with her fingers and stroked up and down his back, he took her mouth again in a desperate attempt to possess more of her. But when her hands dipped below his waist to his backside, he almost lost all control. Her softness against his hardness, her sounds of pleasure, the heat they'd generated in too short a time made him realize he couldn't last much longer.

He passed his hand between them, rolling her onto her back. Stroking up her thigh, then her belly, he was pleased when she moaned against his lips. When he slid his fingers between her legs, she arched against him. She was ready. With his grasp on control a mere kiss or touch away from unraveling, he rose above her. She opened her eyes and their gazes locked.

When he slid into her slowly, she gasped and clutched his shoulders.

"Are you okay?"

"Oh, Lucas, it feels so wonderful."

Her words catapulted him over the edge. With his next thrust, she cried his name, her face flushed with pleasure. Not able to hold back, he thrust again and again until he was no longer a man and she his woman. They were one body and the pleasure was so sublime he gave himself up to it, knowing his life would never be the same.

When Olivia and Lucas walked into Barrington on Monday morning, she couldn't help but smile. She glanced up at her husband and saw he was smiling, too. They'd had a brief honeymoon, but it had been spectacular! They hadn't left the room until breakfast with her mother. Then they'd gone back to the big round bed again until they'd hurriedly dressed for their flight out. Lucas had been so passionate, so tender.

She wondered if the first time had been as earth-shattering for him as it had been for her. He'd seemed to guard himself more afterward, not meeting her gaze in the same way, not letting her see that her touch affected him. Apparently he hadn't lost his desire for her because he'd reached for her again and again. But after that first time, she'd felt the distance he always kept between them. More than once she'd held back an "I love you." She sensed he still wasn't ready to hear it and even less ready to say it.

What if he never could? What if he never loved her the consuming way she loved him? *That wasn't possible*. She'd show him all about love and how it could change his life.

They were standing at the elevator when Cindy saw them and waved from down the hall. Then she beckoned to Olivia.

"How soon do you want to tell everyone?" Olivia

asked Lucas. "My friends are probably in the cafeteria for their first cup of coffee."

He put his arm around her, his hand resting easily at her waist. "The sooner the better."

As they walked toward the cafeteria, Cindy waited for them, noticing Lucas's arm around Olivia. Her friend's brows arched slightly, but she just smiled. "We're setting a time to look for dresses. How does Wednesday after work sound?"

Olivia glanced at Lucas. "That's fine. Is everybody inside?"

"They sure are. Come have coffee with us." Her invitation included Lucas.

When they walked into the cafeteria, there was the usual before-work bustle. Molly, Patricia, Rachel and Sophia sat at a table near the coffee urn. Molly's boss, Jack Cavanaugh, and Stanley stood talking to one side of it, cups in hand. As Olivia, Lucas and Cindy approached the group, Olivia noticed Molly staring at Jack in such a way that Olivia knew was more than admiration or friendship. But Jack acted like a big brother to everyone in his department, including Molly, though her friend hoped for much more.

Cindy slipped into a seat beside Sophia, and everyone at the table stopped talking as they noticed Lucas's arm around Olivia. Even Stanley and Jack were watching.

Olivia didn't know why she was nervous. These were her friends! With a smile, she began, "Lucas and I have an announcement to make."

As she glanced up at her husband, his hold tightened slightly and he continued in a voice loud enough to carry. "Olivia and I were married over the weekend."

Stunned silence met the announcement until suddenly Cindy and Molly jumped up and came to hug Olivia.

"Congratulations."

"How wonderful!"

"How long have you been planning this?"

"Where did you get married?"

Olivia wasn't sure who had asked what. Laughing, she hugged all her friends. When she was finished, she looked up and saw Stanley was about two feet away with a frown on his face.

Keeping their explanation simple, Lucas offered, "We flew to Las Vegas over the weekend."

"A Las Vegas wedding," Rachel said wistfully. "How romantic!"

"It's just a shame your friends and family couldn't share it with you," Stanley observed, then gave Olivia an affectionate hug.

"Mom flew out to meet us," she told him. "We didn't want a fuss."

Stiffly her boss stretched out his hand to Lucas. "Congratulations."

Lucas gave Stanley's hand a perfunctory shake.

Olivia wished Stanley could really get to know Lucas...could understand what a good man he was. But she understood now that her boss was acting protectively on her behalf...like a father. And she appreciated his looking out for her, but it wasn't necessary.

After he checked his watch, Lucas laid a hand on her shoulder. "I have to get upstairs. I'm expecting some calls."

Covering his hand with hers, she said, "I'll come with you."

Sophia shook her finger at Olivia. "Don't think

you're getting away that easily. We want some details."

A blush heated Olivia's cheeks as she thought about all the details she wasn't about to mention. "I'll meet you here at ten-thirty for a short break. How's that?"

"Plans for lunch?" Cindy teased.

Everyone knew Cindy and her fiancé, Kyle, snuck out at lunch to spend time together. Olivia had caught them necking in Kyle's car one day when she'd run errands. Not sure whether or not she'd see Lucas during the workday, she joked, "We haven't planned that far ahead."

After more good wishes, with Lucas's hand on the small of her back, they left the cafeteria and took the elevator to the third floor.

Before they went their separate ways, Lucas clasped her hand. "Come to my office for a minute."

She wondered if he'd been embarrassed by her friends in the cafeteria. But she didn't get a chance to ask as he opened his office door, closed it, then took her into his arms. When he kissed her, she felt all the passion that had enveloped them this morning right after they'd awakened.

He caressed her cheek as his tongue breached her lips, and his hand slipped down her jacket, pressing her close. Just as on Christmas Eve, the taste of him and the touch of his hands swept her into a realm of passion that made her forget time and place. The intensity once scared her. Now she welcomed it along with the raw hunger she always found in Lucas. She wanted to assuage it, satisfy it, to prove her love.

But this morning they stopped with the kiss, and

he leaned his forehead against hers. "Did you want your friends at our wedding?"

It was evident he wondered if she regretted their haste. She didn't. "Mom was there. *You* were there. I can celebrate with my friends now that we're back, just as we'll celebrate with Mim and Wyatt." Lucas had called the ranch as soon as they'd returned. Mim and Wyatt had congratulated them both, insisting they come to Flagstaff over the weekend.

Lucas studied her, his blue eyes deepening with thoughts he didn't share. Then he brought her close for another explosive kiss. When he leaned away, he asked in a husky voice, "Want to meet me here for lunch?"

She laughed. "Lucas Hunter, you don't have lunch on your mind, and you know it."

"What do you have on your mind?" he asked seriously.

Playfully straightening his tie, she leaned in and whispered, "Making sure the blind is closed and the door locked while we eat turkey sandwiches."

His crooked grin stole her breath as he backed away. "I'll be waiting for you."

As she left his office, she hoped she'd continue to hear those words for the rest of their lives.

When Lucas let himself into the town house on Thursday evening, he found himself whistling. He was anxious to tell Olivia about the partnership offer he'd received, eager to spend the evening with her in or out of bed. Last night she'd gone shopping with her friends while he'd made arrangements to have a mover empty her apartment at the end of the month and put her furniture in storage. They'd driven sepa-

rately today because he'd known he could get tied up,
and she'd wanted to stop for wallpaper and paint samples. After they'd returned from Las Vegas, they'd
discussed transforming the guest room into a nursery.
But they might want to hold off on that now until he
made a decision about the job offer he'd received
today. If he took the partnership in New York...

Good smells came from the kitchen, but he found
Olivia in the guest room, sitting cross-legged on the
bed in the midst of catalogs and snips of wallpaper.
She looked up and smiled when she saw him, and he
realized how much he liked coming home to her.
With her hair tied up in a ponytail and in her jeans
and T-shirt, she looked younger than her twenty-six
years, and much too tempting to resist.

When he bent to her, she responded with a kiss that
reminded him of taking a shower with her that morning, the allure of her wet skin and the pleasurable
result of two-for-one bathing. Moments later, he'd
pushed aside the books and samples and undressed
her with the same eagerness that had her hands on his
belt buckle, his fly and then him. Fast. Fiery. An explosion that rocked him and left him wanting more.
He couldn't understand why he couldn't sate his desire or why it increased rather than eased.

As he rolled to her side, catalogs bumped to the
floor.

She propped on her elbow and smiled. "You'll
have to help me decide. I not only picked up wallpaper samples but catalogs with furniture—"

"We might not turn this into a nursery."

"You want to put the baby in our room?" she
asked, perplexed.

Plumping a pillow in back of him, he sat up. "I

received an overnight letter today and a follow-up phone call. A firm in New York wants to bring me in as a partner as soon as I'm finished at Barrington. The founder of the firm is flying in to meet with me next week.''

Olivia slowly sat up beside him. ''Is this the same firm that offered you a job before?''

''Only Rex and Whitcomb knew about that,'' Lucas said, irritated that his private business had been discussed openly. ''And I doubt very much if you heard it from Rex.''

She blushed and pushed her hair away from her forehead. ''Stanley mentioned it. But he said you'd turned it down.''

Obviously Olivia and Stanley had discussed him. Why? ''Am I often a topic between you and Stanley Whitcomb?''

''No! It's just…he was telling me you might not stay at Barrington very long…because you had other offers.''

''And he felt you needed to know this because…''

When she faced him, she answered, ''Because he knows how *I* feel about Phoenix and Barrington.''

''Clue me in, Olivia. How *do* you feel?''

She evaded his gaze for a moment, and he realized Whitcomb probably knew more about his wife than he did! He didn't like the feeling, and it was even more reason to seriously consider the partnership in New York. He'd get Olivia away from Whitcomb and any lingering feelings she might still have for him.

''We haven't talked about my father very much,'' she said softly.

''What does he have to do with this?''

''Everything.'' She sighed.

"I don't understand. Whenever the subject comes up, you tell me you're not in touch often. Isn't that true?" He couldn't believe Olivia would intentionally keep something from him.

"It's true. It just hurts a lot to talk about Dad."

His relief came out as a long breath. Laying his hand on her thigh he requested, "Tell me."

"There's not much to tell. We'd moved to ten different cities by the time I was eight. Once I started school, Mom would put applications in for teaching positions but we never stayed in one place long enough for her to be hired. I always felt like the odd kid out. I'd make friends, then have to say goodbye. It was always so hard starting over...." Her voice caught.

"Why did you move so much?"

"Dad never had a *regular* job. He'd be in sales for one company, quit and start somewhere else. Or he'd start his own business." She sighed and shook her head. "Debts mounted up. Mom worked wherever she could in day care or as a teacher's aide, hardly making enough to pay basic expenses. Dad chased his dreams while she took responsibility for us. When I was nine, she'd had enough. She heard of a teaching position in Tucson. When the board hired her, she filed for divorce."

"And your dad?"

"Is still moving from place to place looking for the deal that will set him up for life. The last time he called he was in L.A.! Lucas, I don't want to move. I like my job at Barrington, and I can have a career there. I've made good friends. I want to put down roots—for myself but most of all for our child."

He sat up straighter, not liking the resolution he

heard in her voice. "Look, Olivia. I understand how you feel. But this offer is too sweet *not* to consider. You would never have to worry about working...."

"I *want* to work. I trained all these years to be a lawyer and I *will* be one. And don't tell me you understand because you couldn't unless you moved around like we did. I need a home, Lucas. A place that I know will always be there."

"We can't have that in New York?"

Her eyes widened. "New York? With its crime and traffic?"

Sliding his legs over the side of the bed, he said, "I'm not going to argue with you about the merits of New York."

"What I think doesn't matter?"

"Oh, what you think definitely matters. But I wonder if you're being honest with yourself about why you want to stay, why you'd want to give up certain financial security for...friends." One "friend" in particular. One friend who would be a nice long distance away if they moved to New York.

Olivia swung her legs to the other side of the bed. "Financial security isn't everything, Lucas. You of all people should realize that. You once told me you didn't have any family. That's not true. Mim and Wyatt *are* your family. They gave you a home and loved you for all these years and will until they die. That's more important than any financial security."

"Don't tell *me* what Mim and Wyatt gave me. I know how much I owe them."

She questioned him over her shoulder. "Owe them? You think they look at it that way?"

Standing, he picked up his clothes. "I don't know, but *I* look at it that way." When she remained silent, he informed her, "We'll have to drive to the ranch on Saturday instead of tomorrow night. I have to fly to Santa Fe again in the morning. I already called Mim."

He'd reached the door when Olivia asked, "Are you still going to consider the partnership in New York?"

"No matter what you think, Olivia, I want what's best for both of us. After the meeting next week, I'll decide."

"A marriage is a partnership, too, Lucas, and if you can't see it that way, we have a problem."

The way he saw it, they might have more than *one* problem. Without answering, he went to their bedroom to change and think.

After dinner Lucas did something he hadn't done in a while. He opened his laptop and tried to shut out everything around him. Mostly he was shutting out the absence of conversation that had marked dinner with his wife. She looked upset. Well, so was he. If he couldn't pry her away from Phoenix, they might not have a future. That thought was as startling as it was obvious. He still believed her attachment to Phoenix had more to do with Whitcomb than anything else.

Finished at his computer about midnight, he went upstairs not knowing what to expect. In the guest room he was relieved to only find catalogs and samples stacked in a neat pile on the bed. She'd looked so pleased and excited earlier to be planning for the baby.

She could plan in New York.

As he entered their bedroom, he saw her propped up and reading.

"I thought you'd be asleep," he said gruffly as he unzipped his jeans.

"I wanted to say good-night. I didn't want to go to sleep with so much unsettled between us."

"We're not going to settle anything tonight unless you've changed your mind."

"Or unless you've changed yours," she added.

The silence between them was as awkward as it had been over supper. When he slid into bed beside her, she laid her book on the nightstand and switched off the light. Darkness exacerbated the lack of words between them as well as the space between their bodies. Ever since their honeymoon, they'd been touching in this bed, or entwined in sleep. He wanted to reach out to her....

Olivia turned away from him.

He forced himself to close his eyes and keep his arms by his sides.

As Olivia exited the elevator late Friday, a stack of folders in her arms, she glanced to the left to Lucas's office. Tears came to her eyes. He'd left this morning with barely a goodbye. It was five o'clock, and she didn't know if he'd return to Barrington or go directly home. Maybe she should leave him a note...tell him what was in her heart because it seemed so hard to do in the face of his determination to dismiss her feelings. After he'd left this morning, she'd realized she was opposed to the move to New York, not simply because she didn't want to leave Phoenix, but because she was afraid if she moved with him this time, it wouldn't be the last.

And she didn't want to repeat her mother's life.

If she poured out her feelings on paper, told him how much she loved him, how much she wanted a life with him...

Once she delivered the folders to her desk, she'd write a letter, slip it under his office door and hope at least he'd be more open to talking after he read it.

In her hurry to put all her thoughts and feelings in some kind of order, she saw the flash of an orange placard to her right, but the Wet Floor sign didn't register until she felt her high heel slip on the tile and her leg buckle. With the stack of folders in her arms, she couldn't break her fall and she landed hard, her ankle turned under her. A stabbing pain jolted up her leg as folders and contracts flew everywhere.

Suddenly the door to Stanley's office suite opened and she wondered if she'd called out as she'd fallen.

"Olivia!" Stanley rushed out, June beside him.

She tried to untangle her legs, but her hip and ankle hurt.

Crouching down beside her, Stanley said, "Don't try to move anything too fast. Tell me what hurts."

"I landed on my hip and twisted my ankle. But I'm scared because..."

Stanley caught her hesitation with June standing over her. "June, could you get Olivia a glass of water?"

"Should I call 911?" the secretary asked.

Olivia shook her head.

When June went into the office, Olivia straightened her leg and blinked back tears, not only from the pain but from her fear. "I'm pregnant, Stanley. I'm afraid I hurt the baby—" His astonished expression stopped her.

Quickly recovering, he asked, "Does Lucas know?"

With her hand protectively covering her tummy, she nodded.

"He *would* be out of town today. Do you want me to call him?"

Bracing herself on her hand, she pushed to her knees, took a deep breath, then attempted to stand. But she tottered when she tried to put weight on her foot and pain shot through her leg.

Stanley caught her around the waist. "I'm taking you to the emergency room. Should I try to get hold of Lucas?"

Remembering last night, their argument, their uncertain future, she finally answered, "He's probably on his way home. And if he's not, I don't want to alarm him."

She was worried enough for both of them.

The drive from the airport to Barrington seemed to take forever, but Lucas had called Rex from the airport and found him still in his office. Better to talk over all the details from his meeting now while they were fresh. He'd write up a report over the weekend while they were at the ranch. *If* Olivia still wanted to go with him to Flagstaff.

When he got home tonight, they'd have to lay all their cards on the table. And he'd find out just how important their marriage was to her...and the vows they'd said in haste.

Standing at the elevator, waiting to speed up to the executive offices, he checked his watch. He should probably call Olivia and tell her he was back.

The doors slid open and Molly Doyle stepped out.

When she saw him, she asked, "How's Olivia?" Her expression was serious.

"What do you mean *How's Olivia?* Wasn't she feeling well?"

"I thought maybe she contacted you somehow...." Molly began.

His heart thudded. "What happened?"

"She fell. June said she hurt her ankle. Stanley took her to the emergency room."

Not waiting for more details, he left Molly standing at the elevator and rushed to his car. Presuming Whitcomb took Olivia to the closest hospital, Lucas sped there, unmindful of the speed limit. If a cop stopped him for speeding, he could damn well give him an escort!

Chapter Ten

He had missed them by half an hour.

His heart pounding, Lucas raced up the steps to his town house. Once he'd arrived at the hospital, convinced the nurse he was Olivia's husband and managed to talk to the doctor who'd taken care of her, he'd learned his wife had been discharged. The physician had told Lucas that she was essentially fine, that she'd be on crutches a few days for the sprain, that she'd been most worried about her baby.

Their baby.

Inserting the key into the door to his town house, he found it unlocked. And when he opened it...

All of his fear and worry and uncertainty coalesced into an almost blinding rage as he walked into his own living room and saw Stanley Whitcomb sitting by Olivia's side on the sofa as he handed her a cup of tea.

"Get away from her, Whitcomb. She's *my* wife."

"Lucas!" Olivia scolded.

"Did the doctor tell me the truth?" he demanded. "Is the baby all right?" He tried to ignore how pale she looked, how close Whitcomb still was to her on the sofa.

"The baby's fine. They did an ultrasound. How did you find out?"

"I ran into Molly. She thought I knew. But there are a lot of things I don't know, aren't there, Olivia? Things like why you didn't call me when this happened. Things like why you turned to Whitcomb instead of one of your other friends. Things like the feelings you have for your boss that didn't disappear with an exchange of rings in Las Vegas. If you want Stanley Whitcomb by your side, we'd better rethink this marriage. But you just remember *I'm* this child's father, and I'll never give up rights to my son or daughter whether I live in Phoenix or I don't."

Stanley Whitcomb rose to his feet, a stunned expression on his face. "You have no right—"

"I have *every* right. I'm her husband. But if she can't put her feelings for you in the past, we'll never have a real marriage." He felt like a time bomb ready to explode, and before he decked Olivia's protector, he had to leave.

He couldn't bear to look at his wife. He couldn't bear to see that she depended on Whitcomb, and that all of his conclusions about the two of them were right on the mark. Wrenching open the door, he heard her call his name, but he kept going. They had nothing to say to each other as long as Stanley Whitcomb was in their house and their marriage.

The slamming door jarred Olivia as much as her fall and, to her dismay, she burst into tears.

"Olivia. Olivia, it will be all right," Stanley assured her as he patted her shoulder.

"He's wrong," she sobbed. "I love him so much. But I think he only married me because of the baby—"

"That can't be true."

"I don't know what's true. Before Christmas Eve, I thought I had feelings for you. I thought you'd be the perfect husband. You're so kind and dependable. But since I found out about the baby, since I got to know Lucas and felt so many needs and wants and desires with him that I want to be connected to him with my very soul, I've sorted everything out."

"What did you sort out?" Stanley asked gently.

When she looked up at him, tears rolled down her cheeks. "You've been like the father I never had. I could depend on you. And trust you. And look up to you. And respect you. But I *love* Lucas. I've tried to show him but..." Her voice broke and she let the tears come because she couldn't even walk, let alone go after Lucas, and she didn't know what she was going to do.

Returning to his office at Barrington, Lucas called Rex and postponed their meeting until Monday morning. Then he paced. Some of the anger had dissipated, and in its place was a desolation that could easily destroy him. He didn't understand it.

After he'd discovered Celeste's true character, he'd ended their relationship, knowing he had no choice. He'd realized she wasn't the type of woman he wanted to spend his life with. But he'd been more disappointed than angry. And he'd never felt this emptiness....

Sitting at his desk, he switched on the computer and stared at the blank screen.

He didn't know how long he sat there that way, but when his office door opened, he expected to see Rex Barrington, not Stanley Whitcomb. "Get out," he snapped.

But Stanley didn't listen. Coming in, he stood in front of Lucas's desk with a disapproving frown on his face. "Are you an absolute fool or just acting like one?"

"If you know what's good for you—"

"What about what's good for Olivia? Does that matter to you?"

"It's none of your business."

"You've *made* it my business. That young lady is back at your town house crying her eyes out. I'm not sure you're worth it!"

He was still in danger of punching out this guy's lights, whether he was older or not. "Look, Whitcomb…"

"No, *you* look, because you're not seeing clearly. Olivia made me leave because she didn't want me to see her crying. She's so damn independent. She wouldn't let me call anyone for her, and she can't even stand with that ankle—"

"You let her kick you out?" He didn't know why, when Whitcomb had the opportunity he wanted, he didn't take it.

"I don't think you know your wife very well."

"I know enough."

"Arrogant SOB, aren't you? Listen to me, Lucas. I've been Olivia's mentor. And her friend. She just admitted to me that once she thought she and I could have more. But since Christmas Eve—and it's pretty obvious from her pregnancy what happened *that* night—she's realized I've taken the place of her father who left on a whim and couldn't be bothered with the responsibility of a family.''

Lucas remembered what Olivia had said about it hurting to talk about her father, how not wanting to move was part of that, and he'd dismissed her feelings because he'd thought there were others.

''Do you know she thinks you married her just because of the baby?'' Stanley pressed on. ''That you want the baby and she's simply part of the package?''

''That's not true!''

''Then why does she insist it is? You'd better think about that, Lucas. She meant her wedding vows. And if *you* did, you'd better get back to your town house and tell her. Or she might not be there when you decide you want to go back home. On crutches or not, once she makes a decision, she'll act on it.''

As Stanley strode out of his office, leaving the door open, Lucas leaned back in his leather chair and rubbed his hand across his forehead. He let the silence weave in and out of him until his thoughts became more clear.

He could vividly remember the first time he'd seen Olivia on the third floor of Barrington. She'd been waiting for the elevator. He'd thought she was stunning with her long auburn hair and green eyes. And when she'd given him a friendly welcome-to-Barrington smile, he'd felt a burning in his chest that had quickly caught fire other places and had never diminished. That flame had leapt to heaven in this office during the Christmas party.

Ever since then, the fire had raged out of control.

And he'd been guarding himself against what went with it. Not only desire but…

Love.

He'd always guarded himself against it because when it was taken away, the pain was unbearable. He'd never forgotten the years after his mother died, trying to make a place for himself, constantly looking for approval. No one had wanted him. Mim and Wyatt had kept him out of the goodness of their hearts.

Yet, what had Wyatt said? *We realize that we should have adopted you.* Maybe they'd truly loved him all those years, not just taken responsibility for him.

Why hadn't he accepted their love?

Maybe because he never thought he'd deserved it.

Just as you think you don't deserve Olivia's love?

Olivia. She thought he'd married her for the sake of their child. Isn't that why she'd married *him*? Yet Stanley had said she'd meant her vows.

Lucas thought about their honeymoon, the way she said his name when he touched her, the way she cuddled near him at night, the way she smiled at him after they made love. Could she really love him as he loved her?

What if Stanley *was* merely her mentor? What if he was simply a father figure and a friend?

Lucas stood and paced again. How could she forgive his coldness…his doubts? Could she ever understand?

He'd *make* her understand.

Blowing her nose again, Olivia took a deep breath and stuffed the tissue into her pocket. She had to stop this. Sobbing wasn't good for her or her baby. And staying here when Lucas thought...

How could she convince him she loved him?

Well, she wasn't going to run. She'd plant herself right here and insist he talk to her, insist he listen, insist—

When the door opened, her heart raced. If she could stand, she would. If she could make him love her... Tears came to her eyes again. There was no way to make someone love you.

His gaze locked to hers, and she couldn't decipher his expression. There was so much turmoil in his eyes. Maybe he'd come back to tell her their marriage was over. She knew she looked a mess in her wrinkled blouse and skirt, her nose probably all red.

Breaking eye contact, she bent to remove the ice bag from her ankle. But Lucas appeared beside her, sat on the edge of the sofa and stilled her hand. "You'd better keep it on."

Somehow she found her voice. "The ice is almost melted."

"How does it feel?"

All the bruises that would probably appear by tomorrow didn't hurt nearly as much as her heart. Tears welled up in her eyes again.

"Olivia, don't cry," he said in a brusque tone, letting go of her hand.

"I'm sorry. I don't know why I can't stop—" She ducked her head.

"You can't stop because you're pregnant. Because I treated you badly. Because you deserve better than a jealous man who's put himself first for too long. You don't have anything to be sorry about. I do. Stanley came to see me."

She looked up at him then, hoping he'd listen to the truth. "There's nothing between me and Stanley. Not the way you think. I respect him. I admire him."

Lucas didn't argue with her as she expected, but held her gaze. "I understand now that you look at him as a father figure. I'm sorry about what I said, about my doubts, about last night and going to bed angry. I know it's asking a lot for you to forgive me. I've been an arrogant ass about so many things. I thought you married me for security for our child—"

"Lucas, no!"

Catching her hands, he held them in his. "Please let me finish or I'll never get this out. My heart's pounding so hard I can hardly think. I love you, Olivia. I don't know how it happened or when or how. But you've become the center of my world. And not just because of the baby. All my life I've been afraid to love. And I've been just as afraid to accept love. I never thought I was afraid of anything, but today I realized I'm most afraid of losing you."

He *loved* her. Pulling her hands out of his clasp, she stroked his jaw with an intimate freedom she'd never felt before. "You're not going to lose me, Lucas. You're the man who fills my dreams and my life. I love you."

His gaze raked over her face, searching for the honesty in her words. Finding it, somehow he managed to shift her onto his lap without hurting her. Somehow he wrapped his arms around her and made her feel beautiful despite her disheveled state. And somehow his lips found hers in an excruciatingly sweet kiss that wasn't nearly enough.

He broke it to kiss her eyelids and the remainder

of her tears. "Can you forgive me?" he asked, his voice raspy.

With tender certainty, she laid her hand on his chest. "Of course I can forgive you. If you can forgive me for holding back, for not telling you how much I love you. Maybe if I had…"

When he brushed his fingers over her lips, he shook his head. "Maybes don't matter." Then he kissed her again.

She realized *now* mattered. And their future. Lucas Hunter wasn't like her father. If he felt that moving to New York would be best for them, she needed to consider it, she needed to show him she believed in his love for her. Leaning back, she said, "Lucas, if you want to move to New York, we can. *You're* my home now. Not a place."

His blue eyes revealed a world of love as he brushed her hair from her brow. "I thought you wanted to stay in Phoenix because of Stanley."

As she opened her mouth to protest, he kissed the tip of her nose. "I know now that's not true. And you're right about putting down roots. Besides, I don't want to live that far from the ranch. Your mother's as close to Phoenix as Mim and Wyatt, and we can have a good life here. You have friends you can trust. Maybe if I relax a little and get used to making connections instead of hiding from them, your friends can become mine, too."

He dug into the pocket of his suit coat and brought out a velvet box. "I have something for you."

Taking it from him, she looked into his eyes.

"Open it," he ordered gently.

When she lifted the lid, she gasped. "Oh, Lucas.

It's beautiful!'' The princess-cut diamond sparkled and shimmered.

"I want you to have something special, something to remind you we didn't just marry for practical reasons but for very special reasons. I want you to always remember how much I love you." He slipped it on her finger above the gold wedding band.

After staring at it for a few moments, she wrapped her arms around his neck. "I love you, Lucas Hunter, with all my heart and soul."

"And I love you, Olivia Hunter, with everything I am."

She raised her lips to his for his kiss, renewing her wedding promise to love, honor and cherish him forever.

Epilogue

The landscape in Flagstaff had changed by the end of April to reflect the birth of spring. Green leaves, the absence of packed snow, the earth waiting for planting, as well as the couple who had loved and embraced Lucas as theirs most of his life, beckoned to him and Olivia many weekends. Lucas had decided to wait until they came to the ranch this weekend to ask his wife a very important question. And whatever her answer, he'd abide by it. Because nothing was more important to him than her happiness...and their child's.

Sitting in the living room, playing a board game with the three older boys, he watched Olivia as she sat by the fireplace with Russ on her lap, reading him a favorite story. Lucas could imagine their child on her lap, cuddling at her breast. She'd had another ultrasound this week at his urging. There were no repercussions from her fall, but as first-time parents, they both worried. This time he'd been present. This time he'd actually seen and heard the beat of their baby's heart. He'd stared at the miracle on the monitor and been overcome with joy. This woman had brought him so many gifts and added so much richness to his life.

Although they still liked to spend most of their time alone, they'd been invited to a party at Cindy and Kyle's, and her friends were becoming more comfortable around him at work. Especially since they'd announced her pregnancy a few weeks ago. He'd even gone out with Stanley a couple of evenings to shoot pool! Olivia had been pleased, and Lucas had realized that, secure in her love, he didn't have to be jealous of *any* man.

Trevor moved the last piece on the game board and grinned. "I won!"

Lucas clapped him on the shoulder. "You sure did."

"Can we go riding tomorrow before you leave?" Jerry asked.

"I'll see what I can arrange," Lucas answered with a wink.

"I wish Olivia could go with us." Trevor glanced over at her. "But I guess bein' pregnant and all, she has to be careful."

Lucas nodded. "I want to keep her safe." Yet he knew he also had to let her make her own decisions. After the ultrasound, she'd told him she wanted to take a leave for at least six weeks after the baby was born, then maybe work out of their home if that was possible. He liked the idea and realized there was no reason she couldn't be a mom *and* a lawyer.

The kitchen door swung open and Wyatt called,

"Snack time. Mim's taking the cookies out of the oven."

Kurt and Jerry scrambled to their feet, and Russ slid from Olivia's lap, following them to the kitchen.

She laughed. "I guess Mim's cookies are more important than the end of the story."

When Trevor didn't run after the others, Lucas knew he had something to say.

Looking down at the game board, the nine-year-old murmured, "I might not be here much longer."

After Olivia exchanged a look with Lucas, she rose from the chair. "I'll see if they need help in the kitchen."

But Trevor stopped her. "Wait. I wanna ask you somethin'."

She sat beside Lucas on the sofa.

"After you have your baby, are you still gonna come here for visits?" Trevor wanted to know.

"Absolutely," she answered with a smile.

"Mim said even after I go back with my mom, I can come out here if I want. I want to see you guys, too. And…I ain't never seen a baby close up."

Lucas chuckled. "You can see our baby close up. We promise."

Trevor's grin split his face. "Cool!" Then he jumped up and ran to the kitchen after the others.

Smiling, Lucas curved his arm around his wife.

Nestling beside him, she teased, "If we don't join them in the kitchen soon, there won't be any cookies left."

"I'll give you something better than a cookie," Lucas assured her as he took her lips in a long lingering kiss that lit their passion as easily as it had on Christmas Eve. Only, now there was a deepening of it that could overwhelm them both. After a last cling-ing touch of lips on lips, he leaned away.

"That *was* much better than a cookie!" Her sweet smile urged him to kiss her again.

But instead of giving in to temptation, he said, "I need to ask you something."

Tilting her head, she waited.

"Before Night Song's filly was born, you heard Wyatt ask me to draw up his will and why."

She nodded.

"How would you feel about me being trustee of the ranch, maybe living here someday?"

"How do *you* feel about it?"

As always, he knew she wanted honesty from him. They'd promised each other that along with so much more. "I think it would be a privilege and an honor."

"So do I," she agreed with certainty shining in her green eyes. "Why did you tell Wyatt you couldn't accept when he asked?"

"I didn't think I deserved it," he murmured, not backing away from the hard questions any longer.

"But you know better now, don't you?" she pressed gently.

He hugged her. "I've learned love has nothing to do with worthiness. It's a free gift. You've taught me that." After he kissed her forehead, he wanted to make sure she understood the consequences of be-coming Wyatt and Mim's heir. "If I accept Wyatt and Mim's generosity, we could end up taking care of children who have nowhere to go. Are you willing to take that on?"

After she clasped his hand, she interlaced her fin-gers with his. "I'm willing to share love and laughter and my entire life with you. And if we can help Mim and Wyatt and someday take over the work they've started, I can't think of a more fulfilling life. I'm beginning to love this ranch as much as you do.''

Gazing down at the woman he loved, he suggested, "In the meantime, why don't we find a house that has an office for you to work at home and enough room for a child to grow."

Her answer sparkled in her eyes. "Maybe even more than one child."

As Lucas bent to kiss his wife again, he sent up a prayer of thanks for her, knowing he'd married the perfect woman for him. The perfect partner. His soul mate. For now and forever.

* * * * * *

Don't miss Molly's story,

HUSBAND FROM 9 TO 5

by Susan Meier

next month's LOVING THE BOSS title,
available only in
Silhouette Romance.

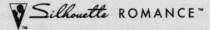

If you enjoyed what you just read,
then we've got an offer you can't resist!

Take 2 bestselling love stories FREE!
Plus get a FREE surprise gift!

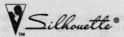

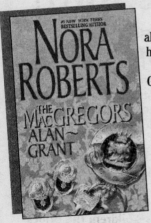
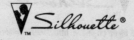

Based on the bestselling miniseries

A FORTUNE'S CHILDREN *Wedding:*
THE HOODWINKED BRIDE

by BARBARA BOSWELL

This March, the Fortune family discovers a twenty-six-year-old secret—beautiful Angelica Carroll *Fortune!* Kate Fortune hires Flynt Corrigan to protect the newest Fortune, and this jaded investigator soon finds this his most tantalizing—and tormenting—assignment to date....

Barbara Boswell's single title is just one of the captivating romances in Silhouette's exciting new miniseries, **Fortune's Children: The Brides,** featuring six special women who perpetuate a family legacy that is greater than mere riches!

Look for *The Honor Bound Groom,* by Jennifer Greene, when **Fortune's Children: The Brides** launches in Silhouette Desire in January 1999!

Available at your favorite retail outlet.

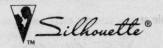

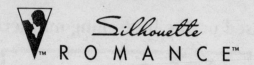

Silhouette ROMANCE™

COMING NEXT MONTH